"Take care of her," ~~her~~ ~~p~~ ~~... ustaf~~ placed Duncan's broken body into the back of his father's wagon.

Duncan had placed his hand on Gustaf's arm and implored him with his pain-filled eyes. "She's headstrong, but she needs a friend. . . . Please. . .promise me."

Gustaf had.

Now what was he going to do? He'd have to talk to Raelene sooner or later. As his three brothers and two sisters, along with his father and mother, stepped away, Gustaf drew near.

Words failed him. The intensity of the pain clouding Raelene's sapphire eyes struck him. But the unwavering jut of her chin told him the fight hadn't left her. She didn't want his comfort any more than she had wanted him. After all, he was just a farm boy. Worse yet. A son who would never inherit the family land once his father left this world.

AMBER MILLER is a freelance Web designer and author whose articles and short stories have appeared in local, national, and international publications. Her writing career began as a columnist for her high school and college newspapers. Her first publication in a book appeared in the form of nine contributions (as a single!) to *101 Ways to Romance Your Marriage* by Debra White Smith. She is a member of American Christian Fiction Writers and Historical Romance Writers. Some of her hobbies include traveling, music, movies, and interacting with other writers. At age three, she learned to read and hasn't put down books since. Recently married, she lives with her husband and fellow writer, Stuart, in beautiful Colorado Springs. Visit her Web site at www.ambermiller.com to learn more or to contact her.

HEARTSONG PRESENTS

Promises, Promises

Amber Miller

Heartsong Presents

AUTHOR'S NOTE:

While the visit of Jonathan Edwards to Pennsylvania in this story is fictional, words attributed to him are taken from Sermon XII, "Safety, Fullness, and Sweet Refreshment to be found in Christ," from *Seventeen Occasional Sermons*.

A note from the Author:
I love to hear from my readers! You may correspond with me by writing:

Amber Miller
Author Relations
PO Box 721
Uhrichsville, OH 44683

ISBN 978-1-59789-939-0

PROMISES, PROMISES

one

Heedless of the home-stitched stockings showing at her knees, Raelene Strattford ran down the tree-lined lane, her skirts flying behind her. Strands of hair from her crown of braids came loose and flailed in the cool breeze. After being cooped inside the house for the past week, abed with a fever, it should have been refreshing, but Raelene was distracted by the lone wagon coming toward her.

It wasn't the one she expected. This one belonged to her neighbors, not her mother and father. One man drove it at a dirge-like pace as another walked alongside, both with heads down. But what made Raelene run even harder were the two workhorses tied behind it. Her family's workhorses! That could only mean...

A sob tore through her body.

Mama! Papa!

Her pounding heart beat her voice dead in her throat, but not the furtive prayers for this *not* to be what it seemed, what she feared. As she reached the wagon, her mouth as parched as the dirt beneath her feet, the driver halted the horses.

"Whoa, Braedon."

Raelene couldn't recall her neighbors' names, not with the panic racing through her mind.

"I am sorry, miss," the larger of the two said, stepping between her and the wagon. The cocky farm boy had actually had the nerve to ask her father permission to court her. What was his name?

5

"There is no way to break bad news," the older man interjected.

Bad news. His heavily accented words halted her steps, as if delaying facing what she feared might change things. But her mind refused to stand still. What would she find? God forbid, they couldn't be dead. They just couldn't be. She wouldn't know unless she looked. But could she bear it?

The wall of a man stepped out of her way. His large, gentle hand cupped her elbow, nudging her forward. With hesitant steps and dread filling her being, Raelene reached the solid wood gate across the back of the serviceable wagon. She looked inside.

Mama used to tease her that she had a wild imagination, but nothing Raelene could conjure in her mind compared to this. This was horribly real.

Mama and Papa lay in the back of the wagon, bloodied and battered. She covered her mouth to catch the moan rising from the center of her anguish, but it escaped. And with it, Raelene's strength. Her knees buckled, and she would have landed on the ground had it not been for two strong arms that held her upright.

"Here now! Do not fall. You are safe."

Bewildered, she looked into a pair of striking and sympathetic indigo eyes. Gustaf Hanssen. That was the name of the man who had disrupted her life last year with his suit, focusing more on her land than on her. The older man was his father, Jarel.

"If you say what you want us to do. . ." Gustaf broke off, awkward, his choppy English making it difficult to follow. He seemed to have trouble only when speaking with her, but somehow she managed to grasp his meaning.

What she wanted them to do? She wanted them to make this go away. But for all the compassion in his gaze, he couldn't do that. She had to deal with this herself.

At the sound of a moan, Raelene shifted her gaze back to

the bodies on the ragged bed of hay and blankets.

They were alive! God had heard her half-formed prayers of panic and answered them.

"Mama! Papa!"

Raelene tried to climb onto the wagon bed but couldn't find footing until Gustaf gave her a boot up.

"Hurry," she told him. "We've got to get them home. . .in bed. . .where I can take care of them."

Their clothes were torn, and fresh blood seeped through the makeshift bandages over their numerous wounds. Neither of her parents answered her call or opened their eyes. They both lay still, but the slow rise and fall of their chests gave Raelene hope.

As the wagon lurched forward toward the house, Gustaf's father gave his account of what had happened.

"Accident. . .horses scared. . .runaway. . .loose bolt. . ."

The words barely penetrated. Her focus remained fixed on the labored breaths of her beloved parents. She wasn't going to lose them. The idea gripped her heart like a vise. No, she'd take care of them, nurse them back to health like they'd done for her on many occasions. And for that, she had to be strong.

Raelene spoke softly to her parents, assuring them they'd be fine, but cut off her words when the wagon stopped in front of the little three-room farmhouse. Puffs of smoke curled up from the chimney, but the usual comfort that filled her at the sight of her home deserted her.

Gustaf lifted her down from the wagon as though she were a doll. Mr. Hanssen descended from the seat to stand beside his son.

"We sent for doctor. I pray he come before—"

"Before what?" Raelene pulled away from the big hands enveloping her waist, took a step back, and shifted her gaze between the two men. Gustaf spoke first.

"Your parents, they are broken inside and out."

Cringing at the thought, Raelene held her ground. "I

appreciate what you've done, sir, but if you would get them inside, we'll let the doctor be the judge of that."

Neither her mother nor her father regained consciousness as Gustaf and his father carried them into the bedroom off the kitchen. Both men ducked as they stepped down into the room. At a loss for what to do, Raelene set about warming water to wash the dirt and blood away, while the men stepped outside to wait by the wagon. It helped to stay busy. Busy meant she didn't have to think about what the young man had said. And she had to keep praying.

Yet for all her prayer, words of comfort, and care, Mama and Papa remained unresponsive.

"They are here, Doctor." Mr. Hanssen's voice carried from just outside the main door.

Doctor. Raelene hadn't heard his carriage arrive. Hope surged in her chest. Everything would be all right. It had to be.

Dr. Schuylar asked Raelene to leave the room. She watched the door close behind him and stared at it. She had hated closed doors since she was little. Even the stairs by the fireplace that led up to her loft had a door that she always left open. Closed doors separated her from the people she loved.

No, she was just being foolish. Raelene raised her hand to her forehead and found it warmer than it should have been.

Lord, this is no time for my fever to return. I must be well for Mama and Papa.

A chair scraped near the stone hearth. Raelene turned to find Gustaf seated on a bench at the small, round table by the diamond-paned window. His father pressed a steaming cup of tea into her hands before mumbling something about fetching someone else. The heat from the cup seeped into her skin. Emotionless, she raised the tin cup to her lips and drank the hot liquid. The strong flavor awakened her taste buds. Warmth flowed through her body, bringing her back to some semblance of reality.

Raelene glanced about the small room, bringing the hand-carved shelves in the little kitchen into focus. In slow order, she saw the whitewashed walls and the cast-iron cooking supplies hung or placed around the fireplace. Minimal personal treasures retrieved from the chests of items stored in the doctor's barn in town decorated the shelves. Papa had plans to build a larger home, and until then, he'd allowed Mama to set out a few things. Her perusal stopped when she again looked at Gustaf.

His brown doublet strained across broad shoulders and barely concealed the work-hardened muscles of his upper torso. The beige breeches disappeared into dark stockings, both covering long, lean limbs. She raised her gaze to his face. Gustaf's chiseled jaw and wide mouth gave way to a narrow nose and deep-set blue eyes.

Those eyes!

Realization dawned on her the moment she caught Gustaf's sympathetic gaze. The memory of his strong arms holding her steady and the piercing intensity of his eyes made her skin tingle. Heat stole into Raelene's cheeks. Why did Gustaf Hanssen have to be the one to find her parents?

"We put horses away and give them food."

Raelene forced herself to focus on his words.

"*Far* go to bring *Mor*."

Some semblance of the hospitality Mama ingrained in Raelene surfaced. "Thank you, Mr.—"

"To please," he interrupted. "I am Gustaf."

But that wouldn't do. She didn't want to give him any ideas when she'd settle for nothing less than a gentleman as a beau. "Thank you, Mr. Hanssen, for bringing my parents home."

She glanced at the cup in her hands. His father had seen to her needs. She should do the same for Gustaf. Rubbing her hands on her skirts, Raelene started toward the hearth, where Mama always kept a kettle of water heating.

"Can I pour you some tea? I imagine the doctor will want

some when he's through. . .and Mama loves tea." She was rambling. She couldn't help it. "She says tea is good for all occasions."

Raelene reached for the handle of the teakettle, realizing too late that she'd forgotten to use a towel. With a gasp, she let it go and jumped away as the kettle struck the stone hearth, splattering its scalding contents. The liquid sizzled on the open flame.

In an instant, Gustaf was at her side, sweeping her out of harm's way. "Here." He took her hand in his. "I look."

Tears that had refused to spill at the sight of her parents' injuries flooded her eyes as the young man blew on the burn. A shiver ran up Raelene's arm, and she tensed her muscles in response.

"You have medicine?" Gustaf asked between breaths.

He had a strong, rugged face, Swedish fair. The room swirled around it at a dizzying speed. Raelene's head felt like she'd been twirling with a vengeance and then stopped to look at the sky. Except this sky churned with dark clouds rushing in from all sides, blotting out the light—and nearly everything else. It made her sway.

The floor beneath her seemed to give way, and she floated above it. Jostled and shifted until her new position became comfortable, Raelene realized Gustaf carried her. The heat from the fireplace warmed her, but she shivered. Gustaf's arms tightened around her back and legs. Raelene leaned against his solid chest, seeking the comfort and strength she had lost.

She buried her head against Gustaf's neck, hot tears soaking through his coarse shirt. Not a thought was given to propriety. Raelene only knew she needed the reassurance he offered. As Gustaf pivoted around the table in the center of the room, the roof began to spin above her, and Raelene succumbed to the blackness that welcomed her.

❧

When Raelene opened her eyes, Gustaf sat in a chair next to

her cot by the back wall of the kitchen. Since her fever, her parents had moved her cot to the kitchen from her bedroom in the loft.

"You are awake. This is good."

Raelene opened her mouth to speak but found her throat dry. She swallowed several times. "What happened?" Even that sounded hoarse.

"You burn your hand on teakettle." He nodded toward her hand, now wrapped and resting across her abdomen. "Your recent illness make you sleep longer. Doctor give me medicine and bandage. You lucky burn not worse."

She cradled her injured hand with her other one and looked away. "Your kindness is appreciated."

"It is least I can do."

Raelene took a deep breath and exhaled. At the footsteps sounding from her parents' bedchamber, memory of their battered bodies returned. "My parents!"

"Doctor is with them still."

She looked at Gustaf. "Mr. Hanssen, tell me about the accident. Please."

Gustaf ran his hand over his mouth and whiskered jaw and sighed. He reached out and clasped her hands in his, as if preparing her for the worst. "A snake scare the horses as your mor and far come from church. The horses kick up and shake bolt loose. Far and I try to stop them, but they run at full gallop. Wagon was not able to handle bumps and holes in road." He paused. "Before we catch them, the bolt came out, and the wagon fell over side of hill. Your mor and far fall down with it."

Raelene withdrew her hands from his large ones. She immediately felt the loss of his warmth and touch, but stared straight ahead. "Thank you," she whispered, growing warm beneath his compassionate gaze. Although the man lacked the polish of her English cousins, he was kind. . .and gallant in his own awkward way.

"I wish I can do more."

The opening of the bedchamber door spared Raelene from replying.

Dr. Schuylar emerged. "Your father is asking for you."

Raelene brightened. That had to be good. She shot to her feet, astonished when she had to lean on Gustaf's proffered arm. With the shock of all that had happened and having barely recovered from a fever, it was no wonder.

"I–I'm fine now," she said to Gustaf, when his touch lingered.

"No, wait." Dr. Schuylar held her back. "Sit down, dear."

"But he's ask—"

"Raelene, your mother is no longer with us."

Raelene sank into the chair Gustaf had just vacated, struck with disbelief. What would she and her father do without Mother? *God, please let this be a nightmare. Please let me wake up and find it's all the fever.*

Dr. Schuylar placed a comforting hand on her shoulder. "There's more, child."

Raelene stared unseeing at the hooked rug she and Mama had made, its pattern nothing but a blur.

"Your mother. . .she. . ." He squeezed Raelene's shoulder. "She was with child."

Child? The word numbed her thoughts. Then the pain resumed with renewed fervor. She couldn't have imagined the situation worse, yet it was. The answer to her parents' sixteen-year prayer also taken away. A tortured sound strangled in her throat.

What kind of God would allow this?

"You must pull yourself together as best you can for your father, dear," Doc Schuylar continued. "I'm afraid he hasn't much time."

Raelene's head shot up. "But he's talking."

"He's holding on for you, Raelene." The doctor helped her up from the chair and led her to the bedchamber door. "God will be with you."

He hasn't been thus far. Raelene gathered what remnant of strength remained, facing the door as if it were an executioner. God hadn't been there for her mother and the baby. He wasn't there for her father. Her father was dying. No, if Raelene had to be strong, it would be on her own.

"Thank you, Doctor," she said, her voice that of an oddly calm stranger. "I know you've done all you can."

Raelene paused at the threshold as if stepping over it would force her to face the cold, hard truth. Her mother and the baby she carried were dead. Her father lay dying. She couldn't let him see her in tears.

Taking a step down into the small room, she walked toward the two straw beds that lay against the opposite wall. A pitcher and basin with fresh water rested on a stand between the beds. Flimsy white curtains fluttered at the windows, but the fresh breeze couldn't hide the smell of death hovering around the room. A lone wooden chair sat in front of the stand, and Raelene approached it. She placed her hands on the back, trying not to look at her mother's corpse.

"Raelene."

Her father's hoarse whisper drew her to his bedside. He lay bathed in sweat, a mere shadow of the strong man she knew and loved. His square jaw was bandaged, and his silver-streaked, dark brown hair matted against his face. The life had all but gone from his light blue eyes.

Raelene brushed back a stray lock of hair from her father's forehead. She held her tears in check. He'd always admonished her to be strong, no matter what atrocities and unfairness were dealt in the hand of life.

With difficulty, Papa took Raelene's hands in his own.

"Oh, Railey," he whispered. His next breath sounded garbled, and she knew their time together would be brief. "What will. . .do without me?"

Raelene tried to choke back a sob but couldn't. "Papa. . ."

He squeezed her hand. "Shh. . .no tears. . .rejoice. Eternity awaits."

She glanced over her shoulder at the other bed. Was that where Mama and the baby were now? "But, Papa. . ."

Duncan followed her gaze and sighed. "I'll be with her soon."

Joy touched his gaze. How could he feel joy in the midst of this tragedy?

He squeezed her hand. "With God. . .we will watch. . .you." A pain-filled but reassuring smile formed on his lips. He winced, and his breath caught. "Our land. . ."

"I'll take care of it, Papa. But I can't do it alone." Raelene sniffed. "I need you, Papa."

Her father struggled to take another breath. His pain added to hers. "Not alone. . .have help."

Help? From where? From whom?

"God. . ." He closed his eyes, then opened them and looked straight at her. "Remember. . .God. . .is with you."

"I need *you*, Papa, not God. Do you hear me?"

He put his hand on Raelene's lap, his gaze fixed across the small divide where his wife lay. "Help me, Railey. I want to touch her once more."

Numb, Raelene took her mother's still-warm hand and joined it with her father's, holding the two together with her own.

She didn't know how long she held them, her eyes squeezed tight against the flood of tears building behind them. Raelene couldn't think. She could only feel the loss of the present and of that to come. It was unbearable, yet she was bearing it.

Bearing it in silence. The labor of her father's breath no longer racked the room. She opened her eyes to see that his eyes were closed as if he'd slipped off to sleep, a sleep as still and eternal as that of her mother. Their pain was gone.

Hers had just begun.

The depth of that pain hit her. She cried for her mother, for her father, for her unknown brother or sister, for the family back home across the ocean. Finally, she cried for herself, for how much she would miss them, for how unfair it was that she couldn't be with them. What would she do now?

Bitterness and anger welled, joining the desolation that filled her. Not wanting to stay in the room where death filled every crack and crevice, Raelene wiped her eyes, stood, and headed for the kitchen. Four people watched her as she emerged, but grief blinded her to their identities.

"They're. . .they're both gone." Her announcement carried a sense of finality, taking her last sliver of strength.

Raelene took one stumbling step before her legs gave out. The crash of a wooden bench reached her ears at the same time two strong arms caught her. Anger at God was the last thought Raelene had before she succumbed to the blackness that welcomed her.

two

The breeze made a sorrowful sound as it swept across the sloping hills and through the bud-filled trees. With the dismal sky, it created a perfect backdrop to the events taking place on the corner plot of the Strattford farm. Rain was the only thing needed to complete the somber scene.

The handful of dirt sifted through Raelene's fingers and dusted the pine boxes that held her beloved parents. A snake, a loose bolt, and a pair of spooked horses had deprived Raelene of joy and sentenced her to a barren stretch of loneliness.

She had cried enough to fill the entire Christina River all the way north to Wilmington and wished she'd died with them. The fever that had kept Raelene in bed and away from church had run its course. She could have gone with her parents, but her mother had made her stay at home.

Now she faced the world alone. The pastor's eulogy droned in her ears, fading to a distant echo as the events of the past two days played over in her mind. The neighbors stopping by with food and words of condolence. The sad faces. Raelene mechanically going through the motions. None of it brought her comfort.

"God is with you, child."

Raelene startled out of her reverie at the voice beside her, repeating her father's final words. She looked up and met the kind eyes of the pastor who had officiated. He had served at the parish in town, but after her family had moved out to the farm, they had switched parishes. Although in no mood to talk, Raelene nodded.

"I'm sorry we did not get into town often. Mama and Papa missed your sermons."

The pastor covered her hands with his own. "Your family is as important to me as all of my sheep. My duty to our Lord is to tend to each one in need. When I heard of the accident, I could not deny your request to come."

"Th–thank you."

"Do not fret, my child. 'Weeping may endure for a night, but joy cometh in the morning.'"

Joy? In the morning? It had been two mornings since the accident, and joy was as absent from her life as were her parents. Unable to acknowledge the comfort the pastor offered, Raelene allowed her gaze to focus on the two pine boxes that lay side by side, waiting to be lowered into the ground and forgotten.

Forgotten by everyone but her.

A tiny box in honor of the unborn child had been crafted and placed upon the one that held her mother. Raelene swallowed against the swell of emotion. Her throat burned at the thoughtful gesture.

Her ties to this land amounted to nothing. What good was a home and land without loved ones?

She tried not to dwell on the bleak future awaiting her, but her mind refused to listen. If she hadn't promised her father on his deathbed that she would fulfill his lifelong dream, she'd have purchased passage on the next ship to return to their homeland across the frigid Atlantic. Her paternal family in England would welcome her with open arms. Even her mother's family in Sweden would be happy to have her, despite their initial disapproval of her mother marrying a man in the British Royal Navy. He would be wed to his service, they had said. Years later, when Papa had resigned his commission, Mama's family had warned her against going with him to a strange land rumored to be inhabited by savages—a barren wasteland sure to kill them all.

Well, Mama's family had been right about one thing. The land *had* killed Raelene's parents. Now she was bound by her love for them and her promise to make something of that land. . .alone. No matter what Papa and the pastor said, she'd do it alone. She had put her trust in God for the last time.

❧

Gustaf Hanssen watched Raelene step away from the three coffins and raise a hand to wipe the tears from her eyes. Just as he was tempted to go to her and offer comfort, she straightened her back and lifted her chin, demonstrating an amazing inner strength.

There'd always been a certain depth beneath her delicate features and feminine ways. It's what had attracted him from the start and made him approach Mr. Strattford about courting his only daughter. Her family had purchased the land six months ago, before winter set in, not in time for planting or harvesting.

Raelene's strength and spirit were admirable in one so young. Other women he knew wouldn't have been able to withstand the funeral service or watch as the men lowered the boxes into the ground and covered them with dirt. Several strands of her honey blond hair fluttered around her face. She didn't appear to notice, just stood like a statue, her face frozen in grief. *And shock, no doubt.*

The small gathering of friends approached and offered their condolences. She met them with cursory responses, her demeanor demure. Finally, his family approached her. Gustaf knew he should probably be with them, but he held back.

"Take care of her," her father had said as Gustaf placed Duncan's broken body into the back of his father's wagon. Duncan had placed his hand on Gustaf's arm and implored him with his pain-filled eyes. "She's headstrong, but she needs a friend. . . . Please. . .promise me."

Gustaf had.

Now what was he going to do? He'd have to talk to Raelene sooner or later. As his three brothers and two sisters, along with his father and mother, stepped away, Gustaf drew near.

Words failed him. The intensity of the pain clouding Raelene's sapphire eyes struck him. But the unwavering jut of her chin told him the fight hadn't left her. She didn't want his comfort any more than she had wanted him. After all, he was just a farm boy. Worse yet. A son who would never inherit the family land once his father left this world.

Gustaf shoved his hands in his pockets, torn between anger and a contrary urge to take Raelene in his arms and give her the comfort she needed, regardless of what she thought she wanted. Instead, he focused on ridding his words of the thick accent that plagued him in her presence and maintaining a respectful distance.

"Miss Strattford, I want to give you my sorrow. It is a sad day."

She peered up at him through narrowed eyes. Not a word escaped her perfectly formed lips. Not a line marred her smooth skin. At her unyielding stare, his discomfort intensified. Unable to stand the prolonged silence, Gustaf cleared his throat.

"You will find someone to buy this land from you, *ja*?" The words came out in an accented tumble.

Wrong choice of words. Fire melted the ice in her blue gaze. Her small hands balled into fists at her sides as she answered with more vigor than she'd displayed since running down the lane the day of the accident.

"No, I will not!"

Gustaf reeled inwardly, the fierce assault of her words battering his thoughts. "Well, since my father owns—"

"I am well aware of who your father is. You need not remind me."

Perhaps the bite to her words was a shield against her true emotions. Gathering his scant patience, he tried again. "But I thought—"

"What you thought, *Mr.* Hanssen," she said, emphasizing the formality of his name, "doesn't matter."

The transformation from a grief-wilted daughter to a prickly rose robbed Gustaf of an acceptable reply. More than anything, he wanted to match fire with fire against the irascible young woman. Forget his promise. He'd head west like he'd planned before being thrown into the middle of this. Let her fend for herself with her high-toned ways. Gustaf clenched his fists and almost walked away. But his strict upbringing stopped him.

He extended his hand to her, wondering if she would ignore it. Should he have washed his hands before coming? Hesitant, Raelene took it, no doubt out of her instruction in deportment rather than because she wanted to treat him with any form of civility. A pained smile touched her lips.

"Miss Strattford, I am sorry if I cause you more grief. I want to say I am sad about your mor and far." At her answering silence, Gustaf made one last attempt to repair the damage. *"Deg Gud till aere oss till gavn."*

To God be glory, us to gain.

Her stony appraisal cracked with recognition of the common Swedish prayer. She tugged her hand free from his, her expression softening. As he turned to leave, he caught a glimpse of tears glistening in her eyes.

Gustaf groaned in silence. A woman's tears were his undoing. Why did she have to show her vulnerability? His words had touched her. That much was obvious. Now he'd have to stay. But he'd have to guard his heart, lest she serve it to him in a trencher. It wasn't good enough for her, anyway.

❧

Raelene watched Gustaf walk away, trying to ignore the distraction that turned her already topsy-turvy emotions over again. His mere presence wreaked havoc on her senses. How dare he suggest she sell her land? Didn't he know she could see right through his words to his true intentions? Just like when he had asked Papa for permission to marry her. He had only his interests at heart. . .not hers. Papa had been willing to agree to the marriage, but Raelene had rejected it.

She noted the broad expanse of Gustaf's shoulders and back

and the inherent grace of his movements. He worked hard but possessed a gentle side. His determination reminded her of her father, although she had never seen eyes in such a dark shade of blue. They showed compassion, then steel. And his accent brought back memories of her mother.

How could she be looking at Gustaf that way? He was only after the land. She'd have to keep her traitorous thoughts in check and remember his true motives.

Raelene inhaled to lessen the tightness in her chest as she stood alone once again on the land of her parents.

Her land now.

The first drops of rain splashed onto her cheeks, the desolation of the day complete. The final words of her father echoed in her mind, but she couldn't give in to the comfort they offered. Even Gustaf's parting blessing did little to remedy the hopelessness within.

As she surveyed the gently sloping acreage, Gustaf's words played over and over. *"Deg Gud till aere oss till gavn. To God be glory, us to gain."* She heard her mother's voice speak the common blessing, and the memory nearly undermined her muster of courage. Surely Gustaf couldn't have known that when he said it. Nor could he suspect the bitter aftermath that now flooded through her.

"Deg Gud till aere."

God, she thought in contempt, the *plop* of shovel-loads of dirt being tossed into the graves echoing behind her.

Give glory to Him? Why should she?

He'd taken away everything she held dear and left her alone on this barren land with no one to mourn with her. If anything, she would survive on her own. She would fulfill her promise to her mother and father.

And she would do it alone.

"Oss till gavn."

Us to gain.

Yes, that's exactly what would happen. She would gain

from the work she put into this land, just like her father had promised. And when she was finished, she would have a legacy created by her own hand. Not God's or anyone else's. Hers alone.

three

Raelene dumped a half-eaten bowl of porridge into the pail near the back door. What little she'd eaten, she'd barely tasted. Although grateful to the women who had brought food to her for the past week, she didn't have much appetite. As owner of this farm, she found that more important tasks occupied her mind and time.

She grabbed her mother's pearl-accented reticule and opened the clasp to make certain the halfpence and farthings were tucked inside. With the land agreement in hand, she headed outside to hitch up the buggy. She stepped inside the barn in need of repair that housed the four horses and two cows, half expecting to see her father busy with the feeding. Nearby sat the pile of wood he'd started to gather in preparation for the repairs.

You have to be strong, Raelene. Her father's familiar admonition made her sweep away her tears with the back of her hand and square her shoulders. A solid barn was first on her list.

She harnessed her favorite horse and ran her hand across the slope of his solid bay coat and over his withers. Like warm satin. . .the opposite of his coarse mane and tail. At sixteen hands and with a wide forehead, strong back, and sturdy hooves, the Andalusian was an ideal companion for her daily rides. It was an indignity to relegate him to pulling a buggy, but he was well trained to the task and she needed a familiar companion today. She couldn't bear to harness Papa's hunter, Jägar. That stud had been with Papa through his British military days. His name made him every bit as much a hunter as his breed.

Raelene reached for Valdig's reins with one hand, touching the animal's soft jowl, and peered into his charcoal eyes. "One of these days, Valdig, this land will have a magnificent barn with twenty stalls, a place to store hay, and plenty of room for a workshop. Just like Papa dreamed." She kissed his forelock, then hitched him to the buggy. "We'll have workhorses to pull the plow and lead the wagon, and you and Jägar will be free to run as you were born to do."

Valdig brushed his muzzle against her cheek and whinnied. Raelene smiled, hungry for affection, a break in the unbearable loneliness, even if it came from a horse. She gave Valdig a final pat and hoisted herself into the buggy. With a slap of the reins against Valdig's back, they set off at a plodding pace down the dirt road.

Almost three weeks had passed since she'd ventured this far from the land. Her illness and her parents' deaths had kept her close to home. With the exception of church services once a month, or every two weeks when the weather cooperated, Raelene and her parents had been storing up supplies for the winter and worked on the farm, erecting the building she now called home. Made of brick and mortar with just a kitchen, bedroom, and the loft where she slept, it was enough to get started.

But Papa had had much higher dreams for the place.

I want to build a grand house with room for social gatherings, Papa had often said. *And it'll have plenty of bedrooms for the future generations we hope and pray to have.*

"Despite your prayers, Papa, you never had that big family your heart desired." Instead Raelene and nine small graves marked by wooden crosses back in England were his only legacy. Yet another request God had chosen to ignore.

The *clip-clop* of the horse's hooves echoed on the hard-packed dirt. A slight breeze whispered through the evergreens and oaks that lined the earth-and-gravel path toward town. Mourning doves and sparrows called out to each other as they flew from tree to tree, some taking food back to their nests for the babies nestled there. Raelene was tempted to stop and pick one of the sweet honeysuckle blossoms along the roadside to scent her purse, but she refrained.

It hardly seemed fair that life could go on so vividly around her when her parents lay dead and buried. It was as if God were adding salt to the raw wounds of her grief.

Besides, she had no time for fanciful dreaming or picking flowers. Raelene held a responsibility normally shared by two people. Working the land to make her parents' dreams come true was all that lay ahead for her.

"Anything beyond that will have to wait."

With a determined set of her jaw, she slapped the reins again and clucked to Valdig to go faster. She needed to speak with the man who held the note to the farm and convince him she was capable of honoring the agreement her father had made. After Papa resigned his commission with the navy, they had had only their investments to start over with in the colonies. Two years later, they had regained their holdings, but the final payments had yet to be made. The sooner she could get to town, the sooner she could make good on Papa's promise.

Lord, I hope Mr. Harvey will deal with—

Raelene broke off the prayer. Old habits died hard.

"You abandoned me when I and my parents needed You most," she said. "Why would You be here now?"

"I will never leave thee, nor forsake thee."

The words floated across her mind like the butterfly that glided over the wild honeysuckle vines. She tucked a tendril of hair behind her ear, vexed by the uninvited verse. It would take awhile to unlearn all the Bible verses she'd been taught from the time she could sit at her father's knee. Her parents had told her the words would comfort her whenever she needed them. But they hadn't. They made her angry.

God's Word was as empty as her heart.

Despite His promise, He'd left her—forsaken and alone.

And He'd left her parents. Their faithfulness hadn't helped them when they needed God most. Raelene wouldn't make the same mistake.

As the edge of town came into view, Raelene slowed Valdig to a trot. The horse's hooves echoed on the cobblestones. On her right, the millinery and leather shops flanked the candle store that her family had sold last year when her father bought their land. Even from this distance, she could smell the wax and hear her mother's words.

"Raelene, remember to dip them in beeswax to make them last longer."

A bittersweet smile formed on her lips. Oh, the grand times they'd shared. Papa had brought them to America in 1736, when Raelene was fourteen, and opened the shop to give them a stable income while he saved money to buy land. Almost three years later, memories were all she had left.

Between the buildings, an alley led to the back doors of quarters where owners lived above their shops—a gap, just like the one that now existed in her life with a door that allowed only pain inside. The candy shop came next. Memories of lemon drops, candy balls, and sweet treats that Papa brought home tied in a cloth almost brought another smile to her face. What she wouldn't give to be that girl again, carefree and so loved.

Raelene clenched her jaw against a quiver of emotion. She had to stop reminiscing, think of anything but what used to be or what might have been.

With her mind focused on her objective, she turned the buggy around the town green. Sunlight filtered through the trees and cast light on the sign placed at one end: NEW CASTLE, FOUNDED IN 1651.

Almost one hundred years later, and despite the progress evident in town, Raelene felt as if time stood still. Behind the sign, several children ran and played. A barking dog jumped in the middle of the melee, causing some of the children to stumble over the furry animal and giggle even more.

Raelene ignored them. The business she had required all her focus. She drew the buggy to a stop in front of the town hall. In her rush to escape anything that might trigger more anguish, her skirt caught on the metal tread as she stepped down, jerking her off balance. She tumbled forward and would have landed on the ground had it not been for the firm arm that caught and steadied her.

"Oh my. Thank—" Her gratitude died on her lips as her gaze met that of her rescuer.

Gustaf.

What was *he* doing here? It seemed like every time something bad happened, his face appeared.

"I have my footing now, thank you." She withdrew her elbow from his large, work-hardened hand.

He called after her as she turned to leave. "Miss Strattford. . ."

Raelene spun around to face him once more. He opened his mouth as if he had something important to say but remained silent. She hoped it wasn't anything to do with selling the land.

"You look well today."

The man was an oaf. . .but those eyes of his. If he could put into words what they suggested, they could make a girl feel like Helen of Troy.

"Thank you, Mr. Hanssen." Raelene couldn't help but feel flattered.

"I say many prayers for you." The sincerity in his voice was unmistakable. Somehow it breeched the wary wall Raelene had built around her beleaguered heart and struck a kindred chord. If she were honest with herself, his face had never been far from her thoughts since the funeral when he'd spoken the Swedish blessing. She no longer believed its sentiments, but the thought behind it seemed sincere.

Or maybe she was so lonely she wanted it to be. She steeled herself. Trust no one—not God and certainly not the oafish man who hoped to gain by purchasing her parents' land.

"Mr. Hanssen, if you do not have anything to say, I would like to be on my way. I have business to attend to and cannot afford to be detained while you founder in your ignorance."

The admiration in his gaze hardened. "Maybe the next time you trip over your feet, I will let you fall onto the street. And"—he pointed toward the commons—"the shops for ladies are over there."

The fluidity of his words made Raelene falter. Then she gathered her wits. "I am headed *there*." She nodded at the town hall.

With what sounded like a combination snort and a chuckle, Gustaf jerked his thumb toward the building in front of them. "Mr. Harvey does business only with men. You are sure he will talk with you?"

No, she wasn't, which made her all the more incensed by this farm worker's condescension. Raelene rose to her full five-foot-four-inch height, chin tilted in defiance.

"Mr. Harvey will see me, Mr. Hanssen, because there is no one else to handle the affairs of my farm. It has been a week since. . ." She couldn't bring herself to say the words. "If I am to continue living in my home," she continued, "I must make certain my farm is secure." She gathered her mother's reticule close to her abdomen. "If you will excuse me."

Gustaf remained rooted to the spot, probably trying to think of something else to say in that thick accent of his; but when she narrowed her eyes at him, he stepped aside. Raelene felt his gaze on her all the way to the main door of the hall. She was tempted to glance over her shoulder, but the idea of being caught looking back wasn't worth the humiliation. She reached for the latch instead. Bracing herself with a deep breath, she stepped inside.

❧

Gustaf watched Raelene disappear inside the imposing brick edifice, into a world that was sure to swallow her whole. One moment, hot and thirsty from his volunteer work on the town hall, he was helping himself to a ladle of water, and the next, he was just in time to save the high-toned little vixen from sprawling onto the street.

Of course, he'd intended to head her off as soon as he realized her destination, but the moment he was confronted by the defiant tilt of her chin and those saucy retorts, words failed him—the right words, that was.

Why had he pointed out Mr. Harvey's characteristic dislike for women in business? He'd started out with a reasonable compliment. She'd been flattered, too, judging by the way pink crept to her cheeks. But the moment he'd told her that he'd prayed for her—and he had—she acted as if he'd committed the original sin.

Gustaf couldn't tell if she'd been mocking his faith or the fact that, in her eyes, he was nothing but a farm worker with no future, unworthy of conversation with the likes of her. That had fired up his temper. And when that happened. . .well, disaster struck.

How would he be able to keep his promise to look out for Raelene when he couldn't speak to her without her mounting her high horse and riding over his pride?

Lord, I know I'm a prideful man, long on temper and short on patience. But You know my heart. Help me to honor my promise, so that I can move on with my life and my future.

Tension slowly flowed out through his fingertips. With it went the clouds of anger and frustration from his mind.

Care, tact, and timing. He needed all three to get Raelene to trust him if he was to help her get her place going. Caring was no problem. At least it hadn't been before she refused his suit. He had to be there to support her, no matter how she trampled his pride. The tact. . .well, he'd have to lean on God for that. As for timing, it was slipping away even as he stewed.

Gustaf stepped silently into the town hall and hoped no

one would notice him. As soon as his eyes adjusted to the dim lighting, he saw Raelene sitting on a cushioned bench across from one of Mr. Harvey's personal assistants. Despite his pinched face and bespectacled eyes, the man could not conceal his contempt. Gustaf took a step forward, ready to defend the lady until he saw Raelene returning the gentleman's disdain with an icy glare.

Having endured that glare himself, Gustaf didn't envy the clerk one bit.

Mr. Harvey approached and extended his hand toward Raelene.

"Miss Strattford, I wish we were meeting under more pleasant circumstances. Please allow me to extend my condolences on your loss."

Raelene placed her gloved hand in the town father's and dipped in a polite curtsy. "Thank you, Mr. Harvey. And thank you for seeing me."

Harvey released her hand and motioned her into the office behind him. "Shall we?"

With a demure nod, Raelene preceded him through the massive oak-trimmed entrance.

Harvey appeared cordial enough, but just before he closed the door, Gustaf caught the patronizing exchange between the man and his clerk. The meeting would not go well.

Although work on the town hall needed to be done, Gustaf determined to wait until Raelene came back out. If she needed his assistance, he wanted to be there.

Aware that he'd aroused the interest of the clerk, Gustaf stepped outside for some fresh air and ambled over to the open window of Harvey's office. Through the plants shading it from sunlight, Gustaf saw Raelene lower her gaze under the stern but sympathetic appraisal on Harvey's face.

Was he going to call in her father's note on the land?

Despite his own opinions about women and business, Gustaf knew he had to do something now. With a purposeful stride, he marched into the town hall and headed past the clerk, directly for Mr. Harvey's office.

"I am sorry, b—but Councilman Harvey was imperative that he not be disturbed," the man blabbered after him.

Gustaf nodded. "I know this. I should be in there, too, and I am late."

He rapped twice on the solid oak door and entered. Ignoring the raised eyebrows of the town elder, Gustaf walked straight over to Raelene. With his most affectionate smile, he leaned down and gave her a chaste kiss on her cheek. Shock riddled her face, blessedly rendering her speechless.

"Forgive me, my dear, that I am tardy."

Straightening, Gustaf offered his hand to the dumbfounded councilman. "Mr. Harvey, I am Gustaf Hanssen, the overseer for Miss Strattford. . . ." Gustaf conjured another endearing glance at Raelene. "Until a better agreement can be made."

four

Councilman Harvey recovered first from the bold declaration. "Well, why didn't you say so? That makes a substantial difference."

Raelene still reeled in shock. Her skin tingled from the brief touch of Gustaf's lips against her cheek.

Mr. Harvey focused his attention on Raelene. "Had you stated you had someone in mind, we wouldn't need to discuss the issue of your marriage."

Just one glimpse of the smug smile on Gustaf's face thawed Raelene with annoyance at the man's audacity to interrupt the meeting and pretend to be someone he wasn't.

"Mr. Hanssen!" she said, clipping each syllable. "I—"

"I do apologize, Mr. Harvey." Gustaf eased into the seat next to Raelene. "I hope I am not too late."

How dare he? Raelene thought, gathering steam.

"Not at all, Mr. Hanssen," Mr. Harvey replied, pausing for thought. "Hanssen. Hanssen." Recognition sparked in his eyes. "Ah, yes. Jarel Hanssen is your father."

"Yes, sir."

"I should have recognized the name the moment you said it. The Hanssen farm is quite substantial."

"Yes, it is."

Had his chest just expanded a bit, or was it her imagination? Raelene wadded her fists in the folds of her skirts. It wouldn't do to speak out of turn and risk losing what appeared to be her only chance to save her farm. Perhaps Gustaf could prove useful, after all.

"I am here to help Miss Strattford."

Gustaf's gaze found hers, and the sincerity in his eyes

startled her. Her heart swelled as if receiving a message meant for it alone: that he cared about her and not just the land as her head insisted was his motive. While the two men exchanged formalities, Raelene sat in silence. She didn't know what Gustaf was up to, but she did notice a change in the councilman's countenance from the moment Gustaf entered the office. Perhaps the respect paid to Gustaf could be used to further her plans.

Raelene called a smile to her lips, aiming it first at Gustaf, then turning it on Mr. Harvey. She imitated Gustaf's self-assured manner, sliding back from her perch at the edge of her seat until she rested against the curve of the chair's back. These land issues must be settled in time for spring planting, no matter who settled them.

Ignoring her, Mr. Harvey adjusted the wire-rimmed spectacles perched on his nose and gave a quick tug of his tailored broadcloth before settling into the high-backed chair behind the polished mahogany table. He leaned forward, and when two ringlets of his powdered wig fell forward, grazing his shoulders, Raelene had to suppress a giggle. This man was all pomp and utterly ridiculous, but he held her future in his hands.

"Now, Miss Strattford, I believe we were about to discuss the stipulations of the signed document and monetary agreement your father had with us," Mr. Harvey announced, obviously for Gustaf's benefit. "Your father was well respected for his integrity and thoroughness, and I have verified from my copy that no aspect has been left unaddressed." He gestured in the direction of the parchment pages she held across her lap. "Have you had time to peruse the nature of the agreement?"

Raelene nodded. "Yes, sir, but I confess that much of the terminology is foreign to me. Would you be so kind as to state the contents in more general terms?"

"I am happy to oblige, Miss Strattford." Harvey adjusted

his spectacles and glanced down at the papers in his hands.

"To please, could I read the agreement?" Gustaf extended his hand toward Raelene, his eyebrows arched over inquisitive eyes.

Despite logic's warning, she passed her father's papers to Gustaf and watched his face for any sign of his plans. The speed with which he read them surprised her. If he was an oaf, he was an educated one.

"May we continue?" Harvey asked with a tinge of impatience.

"Yes, please." Raelene lowered her eyes.

"From the will your father requested when he purchased the land, you are the sole owner, assuming all responsibilities pertaining to the land. According to the land agreement, you will be required to make the monthly payments on the loan, which ends in one year."

"I understand."

Harvey stood and walked to a desk in the corner of his office. The wood gleamed, just like the rest of the furniture in the immaculate room. It reminded her of her home back in England, where her father's position in the British military had afforded a similar affluent way of life. But she wasn't in England. She was in the northernmost of Pennsylvania's three lower counties. And she would transform her family's farm into one that rivaled the Hanssens', with elegant furnishings that outdid their simple decorations, no matter what sacrifices she must endure.

First, she had to convince Mr. Harvey that she was capable of honoring the agreement her father had made.

Harvey perused the loan papers. "Half of the land must be cultivated for crop growth or grazing and be in full profit production for the loan to remain in good standing."

Concern for the undeveloped state of the land caused her stomach to flutter. She had no idea how to ready land for farming other than chop down trees and clear brush. Common sense told her there was more to it than that—more than any single woman could do. "Does the loan provide a time limit for this requirement?"

Mr. Harvey glanced up from the papers, his eyebrows raised. "Do you foresee this as a problem?"

"I cannot say for certain, but we had purchased the land only last autumn and managed to erect a modest cottage of two rooms and a loft before winter arrived. There wasn't time to plow the land or get supplies for planting." Raelene twisted the clasp to the reticule in her lap. "That is why I journeyed into town. I wanted to be certain all of the affairs for the farm are in order and establish contact with you so we can continue the arrangement my father made."

"Please, do forgive my boldness, Miss Strattford, but might I inquire as to your age?"

"Seventeen," she replied, holding her head high. "I'll be eighteen in October."

Mr. Harvey tilted his chin and observed her over his glasses. "Miss Strattford, the assembly is willing to extend a brief period of one month on the loan to allow you the opportunity to properly grieve your loss and make plans for planting season." He stood again and stepped around the table. "Would you tarry one moment while I step into the other room to retrieve additional paper in order to document this alteration?"

The moment Mr. Harvey disappeared, her shoulders fell. When Gustaf shifted next to her, she steeled them, cocking her chin at him in defiance.

"I don't know what you think you are up to, Gustaf Hanssen, by intruding on this meeting and implying there is more to our acquaintance than truly exists, but if you think you're going to gain access to my father's land by pretending—"

"Miss Strattford, it is clear Mr. Harvey was not happy to see a woman in grief or talk business with you. But he gave your father much respect by agreeing to do so," Gustaf pointed out with a practicality that was as frustrating as it was true. "I came so he knows you will be able to do what you are promising."

He spoke the truth, so Raelene forced herself to remain calm. "I am more than capable of hiring the help I need to make my farm successful. But be forewarned, just because your presence here might make Mr. Harvey decide in my favor, I intend to prove that your help is neither needed nor wanted. I am aware of your true intentions."

"If you think you know, good." Instead of being angry, Gustaf leaned toward her, appearing mildly amused.

Raelene's breath caught in her throat at his nearness. He smelled of sweat from his hard labor, but it was a manly scent that did anything but repulse her.

"If not," he continued, "you might need me more than you think."

"I don't need you, Mr. Hanssen—I need a hireling who knows his place."

With a snort that implied he knew more than she, Gustaf leaned back in his chair, lazily taking up her challenge. "We will see."

"Do you have anyone who might vouch for you or act as an overseer to your lands?" Mr. Harvey asked, entering the room and curtailing their debate.

Something shriveled inside Raelene, despite her stiff reply. "Why do I need someone else to speak for me, Mr. Harvey?"

"You are no doubt aware, Miss Strattford, that young women do not normally conduct business and are not involved in its discussions. The situation would be different if you were a widow, but you are barely an adult, and as such, the assembly requires an assurance on its investment."

Raelene met the councillor's gaze directly, hoping the collision wouldn't lead to the end of her plans. "Mr. Harvey, I have no intention of allowing my farm to fail and will do whatever it takes to ensure that."

"I applaud that determination, Miss Strattford, but we cannot always foresee the future. You must have someone who can be listed with you on the loan as an overseer in the event any problems occur."

Raelene opened her mouth to reply, but Gustaf spoke instead. "Mr. Harvey, I think we have that."

"Ah, yes, so you said upon your arrival." The councilman perused the papers on his desk once more. "But that doesn't solve the other matter."

Apprehension increased Raelene's heartbeat. "What other matter?"

Mr. Harvey pressed his fingertips together. "Your father's will contains one other requirement for you to maintain ownership of the land."

"What is that requirement?"

"You must be married by your eighteenth birthday, or you forfeit the land to the assembly, thereby making it available for purchase."

Raelene pressed a fist to her mouth, fighting back the pain that seized her chest. The room and its inhabitants blurred before her eyes. No. This couldn't be happening. This couldn't be possible. Papa would never require that of her. He loved her and the land too much to put that kind of price on it.

"If you were married or betrothed," Mr. Harvey continued, "this wouldn't be a problem. However, since you are neither. . ." He shifted his gaze to Gustaf. "Or are you?"

"No, but—"

"Yes, she is."

Raelene jerked around in her chair. To suggest they were partners was one thing, but this went beyond the pale. When she met Gustaf's gaze, a contrary rush of assurance flowed from it. *Trust me*, it seemed to say.

She wasn't sure she could.

"Mr. Hanssen, I—"

"Please, forgive us, Mr. Harvey." Gustaf seemed to sort out his words before he continued. "We spoke to each other a short time ago about the future. This news brings shock, and with all that has happened, Miss Strattford is not herself. I hope you understand."

Panic seized Raelene's thoughts. Every fiber in her being wanted to refuse the same way she had scorned his offer of marriage last year. But everything was different now. She didn't have the protection of her parents. And if she didn't go along with Gustaf, she couldn't keep her promise to her father. Mr. Harvey would take back the land. But if she allowed the councillor to believe they were betrothed...

She could save the land and break the engagement later. "It—it has been a most difficult time." Raelene sniffed, drawing out an embroidered handkerchief to dab at her eyes. Her tears were real, even if their motivation was suspect.

"Raelene, my dear." Gustaf reached out and took her right hand between both of his, rubbing his thumb against her skin. "The councilman is here for business. We can talk of our future later."

The sound of her given name for the first time on his lips and the warm touch of his strong hands caressing hers set Raelene's reason and emotions spinning out of control. She cleared her throat to speak, but no sound came forth.

"So, Mr. Hanssen, you are in accord to sign your name alongside Miss Strattford's to signify that you will assume all responsibilities should any problems occur?"

"Yes, sir. I am."

"And the details of your marriage will be worked out between you two."

"Yes."

Gustaf's voice sounded strong and sure. Raelene wished she felt the same.

"Very well. Let us proceed."

Raelene watched the exchange in dismay. These two men were deciding the fate of her farm without her say. She wanted to remind them the land had been left to her, but she knew she needed Gustaf in order for her father's dream to be realized. She tugged her hand free from Gustaf's.

"Pardon my interruption, but I need to clarify one part of this arrangement."

Mr. Harvey shot her a questioning look. "And what would that be?"

"While you have made it clear that Mr. Hanssen is my assurance that the land agreement will be honored, the land is still legally in my name only."

"Until we wed," Gustaf put in.

As if that would ever happen. Nonetheless, Raelene summoned a saccharine smile.

"Of course, dear," she said. "But until then, I would like to be consulted on the major decisions pertaining to the farm. I hope not to be considered incompetent."

Mr. Harvey clasped his hands in front of him. "It is not your ability or any lack thereof that is in question, Miss Strattford. It is merely the practice of this assembly to conduct negotiations with men."

"Mr. Harvey, I am aware of the standard protocol. Negotiate all you will with Mr. Hanssen, but solely in my presence. Is that too much to ask?" He started to object, so she hastened to continue. "I only ask out of deference and respect for my father—and the fact that I am legally the owner."

Harvey scowled, clearly vexed at the legal technicality. "Very well," he said at last. "I hardly see where your presence will be an issue, as long as you and Mr. Hanssen are in agreement," he added, with an awkward glance at Gustaf. "And I do not expect that to be a problem, since your father was as practical as he was honorable." The look he sent Raelene's way suggested more warning than observation. "I have no doubt that he would raise his daughter with the same level of honesty and practicality." He gestured toward Gustaf. "Your Mr. Hanssen has been raised on a farm his entire life. He is knowledgeable about the workings of one and will be a great asset in your endeavors."

Raelene pursed her lips, holding back her rankled thoughts. But her displeasure must have shown despite her effort to hide it.

"How much time have you spent running a farm, Miss Strattford?" Harvey challenged.

"Only the past few months after Papa purchased it, but—"

"Exactly my point, and forgive me for interrupting. The facts remain." He released a measured breath and regarded her for a moment. "We do not often change the way things are done. Considering the circumstances, however, we can make an exception. But you must understand this does not negate Mr. Hanssen's primary position when addressing our assembly."

Whether she liked it or not, Harvey spoke the truth. She was no more ready to assume the responsibility thrust on her than she was this new twist fate had thrown at her.

Gustaf shifted his stance next to her. To her surprise, instead of triumph, a hint of tenderness kindled in his gaze. She preferred triumph. It was easier to deal with. That his concern for her might be genuine undermined the foundation of distrust upon which her feelings toward Gustaf were built.

Had she been wrong to judge him so fast? Was it possible that the only reason for his presence today was for her and not her land?

Gustaf cleared his throat, making her aware that she'd been searching the depths of his deep blue gaze longer than was proper. Embarrassed, she lowered her gaze.

Papa, what would you do? Not for the first time in the past week did she wish for her father's and mother's counsel. They had always been there to help with advice and provide answers for her many questions.

It wasn't like she had a choice, reason reminded her.

She raised her eyes to Mr. Harvey, who waited patiently for her answer. "Very well, Mr. Harvey. I accept."

"Excellent. Now, if you both would sign your names to this

agreement, we shall complete this matter and allow you to be on your way."

Raelene stood along with Gustaf and listened to Mr. Harvey briefly reiterate the terms of the agreement before handing her the quill. Raelene dipped it in the inkwell and scratched her signature on the parchment with the distinct feeling that she was putting more at risk than her land.

She watched Gustaf sign his name next to hers. The sight of their names side by side filled her with an odd mixture of uncertainty and assurance. She stole a glance at Gustaf and found him looking at her with the same mixture of emotions. She felt an unfamiliar flutter, although whether it came from her stomach or her heart was impossible to tell. It rose fast, sending her senses scrambling.

What had she done?

five

The morning sunlight blinded Gustaf as he offered Raelene his arm and escorted her onto the sidewalk in front of the town meeting hall. Once beyond the entrance, she cast a glance at him, causing him to step away. He walked silently beside her, twisting his hat in front of him as though it were his tongue. She looked as nervous as he felt.

Could she be regretting her agreement to accept his help? Gustaf couldn't understand why he had offered and why he had pretended a relationship between them that didn't exist. He had simply opened his mouth, and out came the words.

Gustaf had good intentions, but he knew he'd have to prove them to Raelene. Trust didn't come easily to her. That much became obvious last year when she refused his suit and assumed he wanted only her land. Why should she believe any differently now? Why think that he wanted more than her farm?

"Miss Strattford?"

He caught sight of the soft leather pouch Raelene held that contained the agreement they'd just signed. The specifics of the controversial stipulation Mr. Harvey had discussed helped Gustaf emerge from his inexplicable stupor. "Before we talk about work, we need to talk about something else."

Her face paled and her lips parted. He wanted to reach out and comfort her, but he'd be overstepping his bounds.

"I still cannot believe he would ask this of me. Why would he be so cruel?"

Moisture gathered in Raelene's eyes. She tried to blink it away.

"Miss Strattford," he began in a soft tone. "Your far loved

you. He wanted someone to care for you when he could not."

She blinked several times while retrieving her handkerchief to wipe the dampness from her cheeks. "But this gives me only six months! I cannot possibly meet and find a husband in that amount of time."

When she raised her head, dismay shone in her eyes.

Ignoring propriety, Gustaf grasped her fingers and held firm. "Miss Strattford, it is not hopeless. I make promise to your father to take care of you, and I will."

"When did you make this promise?"

"When I find them the day of the accident."

Raelene jerked her hand from his. "So, that is the meaning of all this? You saw another opportunity to get to the land, and you took it." She glared at him. "I should have known you would try something like this again. You were probably waiting for the right moment to pounce. Then you stayed nearby to make sure I would not forget it was you who made it possible for me to keep my land. You probably spoke with Mr. Harvey before I even—"

Gustaf rammed his fist into the nearest tree trunk, startling Raelene into silence. His knuckles throbbed. A person could only take so much. "Miss Strattford, you think me to be full of deceit. But I am involved only to help you. I spoke with others who talked about Mr. Harvey. My father and Stefan know them, too." He ran a hand through his hair and tried to calm his anger. "When I saw you in town this morning, I did not wish to get involved, but I made a promise to your father. I will honor that promise."

He waited for her to interrupt again, but she remained mercifully quiet.

"And to find a husband in six months, that will not be difficult. You are beautiful, and your farm has great promise. You will have all men from here to Philadelphia interested." He frowned. "If they can get around your prickly outside."

Raelene stiffened. "If you think it is so easy, then *you* find me a husband!" She folded her arms in smug victory. "I am not interested in a husband. What I want is to fulfill my own promise to my father and make this farm successful." She extended her right arm in his direction, palm up. "You wanted to oversee the problems? They are yours."

Gustaf opened his mouth to protest, but the words died in his throat. It wouldn't do any good to match fire with fire. Although her body spoke of anger, her eyes showed hurt. He couldn't bring himself to wound her further. But now, not only would he be an overseer, he had to play matchmaker, as well. How far was his promise going to take him?

"You wish me to take care of that, Miss Strattford? I will." He forced his voice to remain even, but his tone brooked no argument. "My way."

&

His way. And just how was she to know for sure Gustaf's way would work? At the steely resolve in his eyes and the firm set of his jaw, Raelene realized he was the only chance she had. In a huff, she marched the remaining steps toward her buggy. Gustaf followed in silence.

She turned to face him as they reached the conveyance. He had returned to worrying the brim of his hat. Perhaps regretting his heated outburst?

His blue gaze ventured to hers. "May I help you up?"

With a hesitant nod, Raelene placed her gloved hand in Gustaf's. She could feel the roughened evidence of his toil through the soft material. These were not the hands of a lazy man. She took small comfort in that.

"Thank you, Mr. Hanssen."

He slapped his hat on his head and tipped the edge of it. "I am happy to serve, Miss Strattford," he replied, forcibly calm.

"Mr. Hanssen, if you wish to address me as Miss Raelene, you have my permission."

Now she'd done it. Why had she made that suggestion? She was inviting an intimacy that could only spell disaster.

At Gustaf's long pause, she wished she could take it back. He must think her brazen, at best.

"I do not think that is right. Far will not be happy if he learns I do not treat you with respect."

Raelene barely managed to stifle the giggle that rose to the surface at the image of his father scolding a grown man. She covered her lips with her hand and glanced away. After a moment to compose herself, she managed a reassuring smile.

"Respect is not the issue. I simply cannot see us calling each other *miss* and *mister* while working together. Not only would it be awkward, but it also would be quite unnecessary."

Gustaf considered the request. "I will think first before deciding."

If only her papa had done that last year, instead of thrusting the idea of marriage to a complete stranger onto her. Had he considered everything, perhaps her relationship with Gustaf wouldn't be so strained. But that was the past, and she had to think about the future.

"Of course." She reached for the reins. "If you will excuse me, I have other things I must accomplish before I return to the farm." She did her best to hide her uncertainty about their situation. "I am certain we will see each other soon to discuss the arrangements that will need to be made."

"Yes. If it is all right, I will come after I finish work here in town."

She drew her eyebrows together. "Do you not work on your farm?"

"Yes, but I work at the town hall to fix loose bricks and anything that is broken. The father of a good friend is a member of the assembly. They asked me to help and"—he spread out his arms—"I help."

"How do you find time to work on your farm?"

"I have three brothers, and Far works harder than all of us. So I can take other work."

Raelene tried to piece together this bit of information

with what she knew of Gustaf from her brief encounters and what her parents had told her about the Hanssen family. He seemed to be a decent man who knew how to work hard to earn a living. That still didn't mean she trusted him.

"I see you this afternoon?"

His voice broke into her thoughts, and she straightened, hoping the warmth that crept into her cheeks couldn't be detected.

"This afternoon," she replied, all business.

With a slap of the reins, she set off for the granary. She was tempted to turn around and look at Gustaf once more, but she resisted the urge. Instead she focused on the tasks she had yet to complete. Something told her that the granary's manager would be no more receptive to doing business with a woman than Mr. Harvey had been.

&

To allow time to gather her nerve, Raelene completed some minor errands so that, by early afternoon, only securing seed for her farm remained to be accomplished. She could have retrieved Gustaf from his work, but pride would not allow it. Yet her pride wilted as she stared at the granary sign overhead.

Bracing herself with a deep breath, she pushed aside the large, two-story door and stepped into the wooden, barnlike structure at the far end of town. The scents of hay and sackcloth filled her nose the moment she set foot inside. Sacks of grain and a variety of other seeds for every need were stacked almost as high as the roof. Wooden rails and thin walls separated the different types of grain. It was a feast for the eyes and nose.

"Can I help you, miss?"

Raelene turned to face a portly gentleman and gave him her most winsome smile. She stretched out her hand. "Yes, I am Raelene Strattford, and I am in need of seed for my farm."

The man took her hand with obvious reluctance. "Henry Borgson." Peering over her shoulder, he scratched the stubble on his chin. "You say you have a farm?"

"Yes."

"Is your husband here with you?"

Raelene refused to be daunted by his implicit challenge. "I do not have a husband, Mr. Borgson. An accident has recently taken my parents, and the farm was left to me. It is now my responsibility to make it work."

Mr. Borgson rubbed his hand across his lower jaw. "Well, I do not normally do business with women unless their husbands or overseers are here in town or have given their permission."

"As I said, Mr. Borgson—"

"Yes, I know," he interrupted. "You do not have a husband. But I am going to need assurance of your ownership. You cannot be undertaking this responsibility alone?"

For the second time that day, Raelene was grateful for Gustaf's promise of help. She withdrew the papers tucked inside her mother's reticule and unfolded them. "I spoke with Councilman Harvey this morning, and the arrangements have been made." She pointed at the two names scratched on the line at the bottom of the deed. "You will see my name there as the sole owner and Mr. Gustaf Hanssen's name as the overseer."

Raelene watched the man scan the document, her confidence wavering. Should she find Gustaf and request that he accompany her? "I do not know what other assurance I can give you, sir. No one in my family is left, and the deed to the farm was signed to me by my father." She clutched her mother's reticule between her hands and held her breath, waiting for his response.

"Hmm." Borgson handed back the document, watching as she returned it to her purse. "If I agree to sell you what you need," he began, looking in the direction of her transport, "how do you intend to get it back to your farm with just that little buggy there? You are going to need a wagon for this load."

Raelene bit her lip. She hadn't thought of that. Having a wagon had been commonplace for her family, but it had been destroyed in the accident. Behind her, footsteps crunched on the mixture of straw and hay, diverting her attention.

Gustaf!

"Good afternoon, Henry!"

"Ah, good afternoon, Gustaf."

Raelene exhaled in relief. Just when she needed him.

"What brings you over here this afternoon?" Borgson exclaimed.

Gustaf ignored the question and gestured toward Raelene. "I see Miss Strattford came for her farm."

Mr. Borgson cast a wary glance at Raelene. The tension was as thick as morning fog.

"Is there a problem?" Gustaf inquired, picking up on it.

Mr. Borgson cleared his throat. "I was just telling Miss Strattford that she would need a wagon to carry her seed sacks back to that farm of hers."

Gustaf looked out the door at the waiting buggy. "Ja, I know this when I saw her horse outside."

Raelene squashed the urge to tell Gustaf about Borgson's other doubts. Besides, Gustaf obviously guessed. The look he gave Mr. Borgson would make an errant schoolboy confess to all his mischief. "That is all?"

Oh, to have the imposing presence Gustaf exuded. Raelene wished she possessed more of her mother's calm self-assurance rather than the childlike uncertainty wreaking havoc on her nerves.

Mr. Borgson scuffed the toe of his boot against the straw on the floor of the granary. "I am not accustomed to discussing sales and purchases with women."

"Her coins are good, Henry."

"Yes, but—"

"And if a wagon is the problem, she can use mine."

Raelene sent an appreciative glance toward Gustaf. Like it or not, she needed him.

"I noticed your name on the deed, as well." He glanced at the two of them. "Is a more permanent arrangement involved?"

"Of—"

"We are still talking about that, Henry."

Raelene clamped her mouth shut, breathing heavily through her nostrils. One more person who would believe their lies.

Mr. Borgson shrugged. "I can accept that." He reached out and shook hands with Gustaf, affording Raelene no more than a cursory glance. "I will sell you the seed you need."

Relief coursed through her. "Thank you, Mr. Borgson. I do appreciate your kindness."

He shrugged off her gratitude as he stepped behind a rough table in the corner. On it sat an inkwell with a quill pen and a box that no doubt held the money he kept for transactions in any given day of business.

"Miss Strattford, if you and Gustaf will look over the bill of sale after I get it written, we will arrange to have the seed loaded."

Once the bill was paid, Raelene waited for the men to load the seed in Gustaf's wagon. His muscles rippled beneath the coarse-looking material covering his back, riveting her attention despite her effort not to stare. That they worked for her gave her a sense of security—the same she had when her father was alive. Not that her feelings toward Gustaf were anything close to daughterly admiration.

They were as conflicted as her thoughts. Twice, Gustaf had stepped in to negotiate when men weren't interested in talking with her. His word and handshake had opened doors that had slammed in her face. She appreciated it, but it rankled her that a woman's word wasn't taken seriously. Then there was the question of Gustaf's motives. She knew he wanted her land—she'd seen the true nature of his opinions in his eyes at the funeral and again this morning before she met with Mr. Harvey.

Once again, she caught herself enrapt by the wide expanse of his shoulders and the carefree manner in which he caught the sacks and tossed them into the back of his wagon. The memory of the day her parents had died, of how he'd held her, carried her in those same arms, took her breath away.

Of course, there'd be no more of that, she told herself sternly. Why she even thought of it was beyond her. Those muscles would work for her, just like her father's prize horse did. Actually, she held more affection for the horse. It had no ulterior motives.

Gustaf dusted his hands on his pants and shook hands once more with Mr. Borgson, then turned to face her. One corner of his mouth turned up as he caught Raelene in the midst of her study. Heat rushed to her cheeks, stiffening her spine as well. Refusing to look away, she read his expression. Cordial enough, she supposed, but there was more—a flash of something that disturbed her. Was it triumph or anticipation? Or both?

"If you are done for the day, Miss Strattford, I will follow you home," he offered with a gesture toward her horse, who stood waiting patiently. "We will get the seed to your farm."

Raelene decided to allow him his peacock-proud moment. He might have rescued her, but he didn't own her, and he'd never own her land. "Very well, Mr. Hanssen. I will see you there."

She headed for her buggy and grabbed hold of her skirts to climb aboard. Once again, Gustaf was right there to assist her. She accepted his hand and settled onto the leather seat. With the reins held loosely between her fingers, she dismissed him with a nod and called to the horse to head home.

Behind her, Gustaf called to his own pair of steeds. By the time Raelene reached the edge of town, the man had caught up with her.

Her thoughts tumbled into a quandary of emotion during the hour-long journey to her farm. She should be comforted by the man's support, but needing him was not only humiliating; it was alarming.

A knot formed in Raelene's stomach, pulled tight by the conflict. The only relief came from the knowledge that, while nothing had turned out as she'd planned, thus far, she still had her land and the seed that would make it prosper. Whatever his intentions, Gustaf was no more than the means and muscle to ensure her parents' dream came true. Nothing more, nothing less.

six

Gustaf grabbed the first sack of seed.

"You can stack it there." Raelene pointed to the only empty part of the wall inside the cramped barn.

He tossed it on the ground, glancing at the cows and the horses Raelene had just led to the troughs. At least the animals received sufficient care. And this land gleamed with promise. His senses came alive at the prospect awaiting him. Anticipating the end result made him want to get to work right away. But first things first. He turned back to his wagon to unload the remainder of the seed.

Raelene had disappeared around the front of the small, thatch-roofed cottage she called home. She certainly didn't live a privileged existence, despite the money he knew was available from her inheritance. The modest shelter and the serviceable barn proved she'd been raised to use only what she needed. But that would soon change when she received a return on her investment. She had to turn a profit, or she'd lose the land. And from the few words Raelene's father had spoken after the wagon accident, he knew that profit would be put to good use. He could see it in his mind's eye. The big house, the two-story barn, the fields full of corn and beans as far as the eye could see. Or were those Gustaf's dreams?

The thrill of excitement dwindled with the reminder that none of this was his. He was simply the hired help and overseer. Neither the farm nor the decisions were his.

Raelene owned the land.

His name might be on the agreement, but she had final approval on what was to be done with it. He'd have to tread lightly. Gustaf couldn't plow his way through and hope she'd follow blindly. No, if he could trust his hunch—and he usually could—this young woman would prove to be quite adept at handling the responsibility dumped upon her delicate shoulders—shoulders with an inner strength that attracted him.

That kind of strength came from only one source, and despite her anger in the wake of her parents' deaths, Gustaf knew Raelene would find it again. His own offer to help had stemmed partly from his desire to see her lean on God once more. She'd live a very lonely existence otherwise.

"Can I offer you tea or coffee before we discuss our arrangement?"

Raelene's melodic voice broke through his pensive state. He raised his head to see the young woman standing not five feet away.

Gustaf straightened, wiping his forehead. Despite the chill in the air, beads of sweat had formed on his face and neck. Refreshment sounded as good to his ears as a dip in the creek.

"Yes." He nodded. "Thank you."

"Do please come inside when you are finished, and we can discuss pertinent details over some cookies and tea."

Gustaf watched Raelene's graceful retreat until she disappeared around the corner. By the time the wooden front door creaked open and closed, he was back at work with renewed gusto. Once finished, he made certain the sacks wouldn't topple over, then headed for the front of the house. It took a moment for his eyes to adjust to the darker interior, but he soon recognized the ample kitchen with a doorway that led into the bedroom off the side where Raelene's parents had died. Next to the fireplace, an open door revealed the stairs that led up to the loft. Nothing fancy, but suitable for the needs of the Strattford family, as they had been.

"Please sit down," Raelene invited, her voice betraying her nervousness.

Gustaf took a seat at the hand-sawn log table in the center

of the kitchen. Raelene removed the muslin wrapping from a wooden trencher of cookies and placed the platter and a tin cup full of steaming tea in front of him.

"Thank you. They smell good." Gustaf sank his teeth into the chewy treat. Delicious! "When you have time to make these?" His accent and stilted words surfaced again. Why couldn't he speak coherently around her?

"I baked them this morning before I headed into town. Mother always kept a small basket of cookies around the house. Father loved to sneak one or two each time he came in from working outside." A wistful look crossed her face.

Gustaf blew on the hot tea before taking a drink, drawing her attention back to the present. "Your mother taught you well."

A sheen formed in her eyes. She blinked several times to clear the tears, but a pleased expression remained. Raelene took her seat opposite him and placed her hands around the tin cup in front of her. She started to chew on her lower lip, her brow drawn in contemplation.

"I wanted—"

"We need—"

They both stopped and laughed as their words tumbled out on top of each other's.

"You begin," Gustaf said.

Raelene offered a halfhearted smile. "I wanted to discuss how we would work things from this point forward." She twisted the cup in her hands but maintained her focus on his face. "You have made an offer to help, and I need to hear what you have in mind." Her gaze shifted toward the window. "You have no doubt seen the amount of work that needs to be done. But you also have work on your father's farm, and I do not wish to keep you from that."

"It is good to have brothers to share the work. Stefan, the oldest, does the most. My two younger brothers help where needed." Gustaf took another bite and washed it down with a gulp of tea. "Yes, I have my job, but there is no problem for me to spend half my day here and half at home. Mor and Far will not turn away from helping a neighbor in need."

"That solves the problem of time." Satisfaction relaxed her worried brow for a moment before it creased again. "What about the order in which we complete what needs to be done? Should not we make a list and divide the tasks according to our abilities? I am not as strong as you are. Neither am I too fragile to work."

Raelene was direct. Gustaf admired that. "Ja, that will be good for most things, but first we need a better barn for your animals and more solid shelter for the grain we harvest when it is ready."

"How will we do that alone? Repairing a barn takes many days or a rather large number of workers. We have neither."

"We have workers. We only need to ask."

"Who?"

"My family will help. The five of us, my brothers and father and me, built our barn in three days after getting the materials. We will do the same for you."

Suspicion flickered in the beguiling blue of his companion's gaze. "I do not wish to be indebted to your family."

Or was it stubborn pride? "We are neighbors." Gustaf brushed off her protest with a wave of his hand. "It is what we do. Help each other in time of need." She started to say something, but he cut her off. "If you want more workers, we can ask others and have the barn ready in one day. Food, drink, and music will follow."

Raelene considered his suggestion, the thoughtful purse of her lips making it difficult for Gustaf to think business. "Very well," she agreed. "Not only would the barn be built sooner, but it would give me a chance to visit with those who live nearby and thank them for their kindness after. . ." Her voice caught. "Well, you know. I have not called on anyone recently. It was always a favorite pastime of Mother's." She squared her shoulders as if shaking off melancholy before it set in. "What about the planting?"

What kind of life had Raelene lived before coming to the colonies? Obviously privileged. That was clear by her speech and mannerisms. Was she ready for this?

Gustaf set down his cup and rested his forearms on the hand-planed surface of the table. "I will bring my horses to help. They know what to do, and they work hard. They will be a good example to your two workhorses." Seeing Raelene bristle, he added hastily, "Planting is not easy. You have a big burden now. You do not need more."

"I am not afraid of hard work, Mr. Hanssen."

"I did not say that, but some things a man should do. As a woman, you can—"

"I can do more than knit, bake, fetch the milk and eggs, and other common tasks."

He took a drink of tea, now at a temperature that wouldn't burn his tongue. "They are not so common when you work all day and come home tired and hungry. It is like rain after a drought." He reached for a cookie to demonstrate his point. "Learning to work a field will take time; time we do not have."

She placed her hands flat on the table, sparks flashing in her ice blue gaze. "Mr. Hanssen," she seethed, "if you are not willing to accept my help, I will find someone who will."

An equal fire kindled in Gustaf. He stood to gain nothing by working her farm, yet she treated him as dispensable as yesterday's slops. He held back the sharp retort on the tip of his tongue and prayed for guidance. He'd had encounters with difficult people before, but Raelene Strattford tested his patience like no other. Fulfilling a promise almost wasn't worth this. But he would stay. He owed it to her father.

Releasing a deep breath, Gustaf raised his gaze to Raelene's. "That is not what I mean. You should learn all you need to make your farm a good one. Get a list, and divide the tasks as you wish."

Confusion softened the tension in her jaw and glare in her eyes. "As I—"

"Miss Strattford," Gustaf interrupted, "I wish for you to do the lighter work for a selfish reason."

Raelene narrowed her eyes.

"Do you know what will happen if people learn I work here but you do more hard work? With five strong men on the farm next to yours? I will bring shame on my family and lose my skin while living if I let that happen. You might want that, but I like my skin where it is."

The ghost of a smile teased the corner of Raelene's lips. At least he was getting through to her sense of humor, even if he hadn't gotten the expression right.

"Mr. Hanssen, I do apologize for appearing to take control. Father said it is one of my worst faults. I get excited about a project and charge into it at a full gallop. I inherited the fault from him." She extended a hand toward him. "Please, accept my apology."

Gustaf reached for her hand, clasping it in his larger one. He squeezed firmly, but just as he started to let go, a soft light flashed in Raelene's eyes, rendering him motionless. Gone was the animosity. Warmth replaced coldness, and he grew lost in their depths.

How long he remained that way, he had no idea. Perhaps it was the collapse of coals in the fireplace that stirred him from the trance. He cleared his throat and withdrew his hold on Raelene's hand. Heat crawled up his neck. "I. . .uh. . . accept apology," he stammered. She could be agreeable when she tried. *Even more,* he thought, glancing away to rein in his errant thoughts.

seven

Two days later, Raelene sat opposite Gustaf on the grass as they finished their midday meal. Although she'd protested initially, he said it was the best time for them to discuss business. Yesterday, they'd managed to determine their immediate needs for the barn and agree on a plan of action. Today, they needed to plan for the food and music afterward.

She speared a forkful of potato and took a bite. The end of the harvest couldn't come soon enough. Fresh fruits and vegetables would be in abundance for winter preservation. At least the garden she and Mama had planted was showing signs of producing well. Her mouth watered in anticipation of the savory delights she'd have at her fingertips.

Gustaf took the last bite of roasted chicken and wiped his mouth. That feisty young hen had pecked at her feet one too many times. Thankfully, Gustaf had lowered the ax for her. "Very good." He patted his stomach and stretched. "It is the right amount to give me energy that lasts the rest of the day."

Raelene warmed under his praise and stood to gather the trenchers. He'd suggested they use just one, but she couldn't bring herself to share with him. That would be far too intimate. What was one extra thing to wash? Because she'd been a willing student under her mother's tutelage and the lessons offered by their cook back home in England, she could at least pretend to enjoy the chores of cooking and cleaning. She knew what was expected of her, even if books appealed to her more. Retrieving the kettle from the hook over the fire, she stepped back outside and refilled Gustaf's cup.

"Have you made a list of what food the other families can bring when we repair and expand your barn? You can save a lot of work if you let other women help." He took a long drink. "You only need to provide the fireplace and cooking area."

"I am well aware of what is involved in planning a social gathering of several families. Mama and I worked together with our cook in England when friends came calling. And we had some small dinners in our home above the candle shop after first moving here. I often read selections from our book collection for entertainment, but I am sure we can find other options. Maybe I should unpack Mama's china—"

"This is not a fancy event like you know from England or with the landowners and businessmen in town. These are farmers and their families. Simple." He shrugged. "They do not need much. A fiddler to play. But no china. It will get broken and look like you want to show off your fine things."

Raelene clenched her teeth. "I realize life here is different from that in England and how we lived in town. I merely wish to appear civilized. My father was a member of the British military, and here he was respected. I want this to be special."

Gustaf rested his forearms on his knees. "We do not have all the fancy things, but we *farmers* can have a good time."

Raelene bristled at the emphasis he placed on "farmers." Still, he made a good point. These people wouldn't be looking for anything on a grand scale. Good food, good music, and a break from their everyday lives. "Very well. I will agree to work with you on the details. I'm sure we can come up with just the right balance."

Raelene stepped toward the side of the house for access to the pump Papa had constructed as their water source. Placing the pail underneath, she cranked the handle up and down. When the pail was full, she walked inside and transferred the water to the basin to wash dishes.

Gustaf placed his hand on her arm, startling her. "To please, I will do that."

How had he come inside without her hearing him? And a man? Do the washing?

"You talk of books." Gustaf gestured toward the shelf behind the table. "Pick one and read. I wash."

It was more of a command than a request, but he spoke with such gentleness, she obeyed. Wondering what he was up to, she scanned the titles of the books on her shelf. Whatever it was, this turn of events delighted her. After picking out one of her favorite books, she pulled the rocking chair closer to the fireplace and sat down.

"I have chosen *Don Quixote*, written by Miguel de Cervantes," she said, running her hand over the smooth cover. "It is about a knight full of dreams, who sets out on his old horse Rosinante to seek adventure, and about the materialistic squire who accompanies him from one failure to another. Their relationship, although they argue most fiercely, is ultimately founded upon mutual respect."

"I think I understand that." Gustaf peered at her over his shoulder, the corners of his mouth turned up and a twinkle in his eye.

Respect? Was he saying he respected her despite their arguments? Flustered, Raelene wet her lips and prepared to read.

" 'In a village of La Mancha. . .'"

Raelene read the opening lines, the familiarity soothing her like nothing else could.

" 'He had in his house a housekeeper past forty, a niece under twenty, and a lad for the field and marketplace, who used to saddle the hack as well as handle the bill-hook.'"

"We can use this around the farm. Ja?"

Raelene raised her head, scowling. "Are you going to make a comment at every pause?"

"I am sorry. Please, to continue."

" 'The above-named gentleman whenever he was at leisure. . . sold many an acre of tillageland to buy books of chivalry to read, and brought home as many of them as he could get.'"

Gustaf chuckled. "This is like you."

Raelene smiled. Perhaps they could learn to work together, she mused, returning to the story. Several pages later, as he finished washing and she came to a stopping point, he commented again.

"You have nice voice. Good to make babies sleep."

She placed the marker in the book and returned it to the shelf without a word. She had nothing to say. Mumbling an excuse about needing to tend to the horses, she fled. But his remark stayed with her.

⁂

Raelene almost couldn't believe her eyes. Gustaf had been right about the local response. Once the call had gone out to their neighbors for assistance, the affirmative replies came to a one.

They had arrived that morning, the men with their tools and the women with their many baskets of food, all more than eager to work. Gustaf had laid out the lumber he and some other men had felled earlier that week, and the men set to work. She spent all day with the women, completing the daily tasks around the farm and sharing in the companionship. By noon, the barn's frame was reinforced, and everyone took a break for dinner. By dusk, the roof had been repaired and the walls had been expanded.

With the work behind them, everyone gathered inside the barn to celebrate its completion.

Raelene stood in the main doorway, dumbstruck with gratitude and wonder. A handful of ladies who formed a society to assist needy families had insisted on serving the food and drink, while Gustaf's two younger brothers provided entertainment on the flute and bassoon. The special performance created a festive atmosphere, and the camaraderie dispelled Raelene's fear of facing the world alone, making her feel a part of something intangible, something that surrounded her heart with warmth.

"Do I find some men to bring in your harpsichord so you can play, too?"

Raelene turned abruptly to see Gustaf standing beside her. "I do not think that is necessary, Mr. Hanssen. Your brothers are doing a fine job."

"But more music is good, Miss Strattford. Your friends have worked hard. They deserve the most. Ja?" A smirk formed on his lips. "And you can show your talent with music to the men without wives here tonight."

Raelene's earlier warmth vanished. For a while, she'd forgotten the marriage requirement. Must Gustaf remind her of the reality of her circumstances every time they spoke? Now, instead of neighbors, she saw married and unmarried guests. That Gustaf suggested she perform like a trick horse to win a man's favor was humiliating. Why had she ever forced him into the role of choosing that man?

"Very well, Mr. Hanssen," she grated out. "If you believe my playing the harpsichord would add to this evening, you may arrange for it to be brought over from the house." He started to leave, but she placed a hand on his arm. His muscles flexed under her fingers as if he was responding to her touch, and it captured her attention for a fleeting moment. Now, what was she about to say? Oh, the harpsichord. "Do be careful, please. It belonged to my mother, and Father moved heaven and earth to purchase it for her."

"It will be safe." He raised his free arm and settled an open palm across his chest. "I promise."

As Gustaf departed, Raelene dwelled on his final word. *Promise.* Why did it seem to be a word that determined so much of what she did? She was running a farm, working with a man she'd rather see as far away from her as possible, and forced to find a husband before she turned eighteen. Why? Because of a promise.

She had promised her parents she'd take care of the farm

and see their dream fulfilled. Gustaf had promised her father he'd take care of her. Her father had required that she promise her life to a man or she'd lose the farm. And she'd made Gustaf promise to find her a husband. What should be a word reflecting joy was shrouded in dread. Motion from behind her drew Raelene from her thoughts as Gustaf's older brother and father approached with her mother's harpsichord. *No going back now*, she thought, stepping aside. Every eye in the room was on her, expectant.

Assuming the proper posture instilled in her from a young age, Raelene followed Mr. Hanssen and Stefan to the area where the younger Hanssen sons entertained with their playing.

She tried to block out everyone as conversations hushed and they watched the progression toward the other end of the barn. What would she play?

A strange sense of panic shoved her repertoire just beyond retrieval. Buying time to collect herself, Raelene arranged her gown to position herself on the bench. But the long train that hung from her shoulders caught under her backside, pulling her shoulders back beyond the line of comfort. Heat rushed to her face. Raelene rose up sufficiently to adjust the problem and gave her lappet cap a nervous pat, just in case the jerk had loosed her hair from underneath.

A minuet. That was the trick. One of her favorites came to mind. As the tune began to play through her mind, she transferred it to the instrument, crisp, dipping, turning notes that conjured pictures of satin gowns, elegant gentlemen in rich brocades, and a far happier time.

❧

Gustaf stood off to the side and observed Raelene. He leaned against the wall with his arms folded across his chest, feigning disinterest. Although everyone in the room listened in rapt attention, he didn't want to reveal his inner feelings to anyone who might see. His eyes always betrayed him, or so his mother often teased.

Far be it that anyone see what the soft strains of the music that flowed from Raelene's graceful fingers stirred in his soul. How he longed for a place where birthrights, promises, stipulations, and heartache didn't exist. A place where he could allow his thoughts to run free and entertain the possibility of things that would never be.

From the look on Raelene's face, the music took her to another place, as well. Gone was her poorly masked nervousness, replaced by peaceful joy. The thin, bloodless line of her lips had ripened to a serene smile, and the soft lines of her brow had faded, giving up their worry and anger.

"She is lovely, isn't she?"

Gustaf turned his head to find the son of a neighboring farmer watching Raelene with undisguised interest. A twinge of annoyance crept to the surface, but he held it at bay. He tried to think of a reason to dissuade the young man, but honor demanded that Gustaf consider him as a potential suitor for Raelene.

"Yes, she is." He focused again on Raelene, overcoming his reticence to fulfill his role of finding her a good husband, so that he might keep his promise to her father and be done with her and her farm once and for all.

"She is a good cook and makes a home very nice," he added in a stilted voice.

The young man turned to face Gustaf. "And how might you be acquainted with this enchanting mistress?"

Gustaf extended his hand. "I am Gustaf Hanssen. I live on the next farm, but I work as overseer for Miss Strattford."

The young man returned the handshake. "Erwin Murphy. I live down near the river."

"How did you learn about this event?"

"My father's involvement in the community is substantial. When word reached us of the need to have a barn repaired and enlarged, we could not ignore the request."

Erwin directed his attention to Raelene with renewed admiration. "Now that we are here, I am glad we came. I would not have wanted to miss hearing this charming young woman play so beautifully." Obviously enthralled, Erwin stepped closer. "Tell me, as her overseer, what do you know about her?"

Gustaf resisted the urge to walk away. It was his duty to hear the man out.

Erwin continued. "I am acquainted with her parents' tragedy. But does she have any other family or anyone who might come to live with her?"

Gustaf took a deep breath and exhaled, as though that might rid him of this urge to punch the man in the face for what he was clearly thinking. But Murphy was a man of property, a good prospect for Raelene. Gustaf slid his hands into the pockets of his pants, lest they take on a will of their own and end the matter then and there.

"It is sad, but when her parents died, they left Miss Strattford alone. They came here from England when Miss Strattford was fourteen, leaving their other family behind. Mr. Strattford did well in business and bought this land, but there was not enough money to bring their other family here." Gustaf paused, grappling with the increasing interest developing in Murphy's gaze.

"Mr. Strattford kept to himself. He traded with farms in the area, and they went to the nearby church when they were able." He followed Murphy's attention to where Raelene played with featherlight fingers. "Mr. Strattford maintained order in his home, and his wife and daughter respected him like he was the head of the British army. More than that, I cannot offer."

Erwin didn't respond. For a moment, Gustaf wondered if the man had heard a word he'd said.

"Miss Strattford is a vision, isn't she?" he said at last.

Not wanting to fan the fire of interest in Erwin's gaze any further, Gustaf held back his full agreement.

"I must learn more about her, speak to her." The other man reached for his watch fob tucked into a small pocket on the front of his vest. "Might you be able to assist me?"

"Ja, I am able to make introductions."

"That would be perfect. Thank you."

Gustaf clenched his fists in frustration. A promise was a promise. But when he'd made it, he didn't know it was going to be so hard to keep.

eight

When Raelene finished playing, a round of applause echoed to the wooden rafters of the refurbished barn. Gustaf admired her demure smile, as ladylike as the graceful curtsy she offered in response. When she stepped away from the harpsichord, he made his move.

"Mr. Murphy," he said to his companion, "please come with me, and I will make introductions."

Murphy lit up like one of the lanterns overhead. "Gladly."

Although he was a shorter man than Gustaf, Erwin's eager strides matched his. As they approached Raelene, Gustaf's heart seemed to recoil. Could he carry this out? The slight curve of Raelene's lips as she turned and saw him almost made him lose his nerve. But it was too late. Besides, this was what he wanted, what he and Raelene both wanted. Wasn't it?

"Miss Raelene Strattford, I introduce Mr. Erwin Murphy," he said, his voice as stiff as the barn's beams. "His father owns a farm near the river."

Raelene extended a slender arm, her palm downward. "Mr. Murphy."

Clasping her fingers lightly, Erwin placed a kiss just above her hand. "It is a pleasure to meet you, Miss Strattford. Your performance on the harpsichord was beautiful. It added so much to the enjoyment of the evening."

"Thank you, Mr. Murphy. I am delighted that you enjoyed it."

Erwin straightened to his full height as though gathering his nerve. "Forgive me if I am being presumptuous, but might I have the honor of calling on you next week? I would greatly like to learn more about you and this wondrous piece of land that is your farm."

Feeling conspicuous in spite of stepping a short distance away, Gustaf shifted from one foot to the other. He didn't want to leave them alone. His sense of honor to Raelene, as well as to his promise, made him stay.

From all appearances, Raelene seemed to be interested in what Erwin had to say. Well, not quite all. Gustaf had been around her enough to know that her rigid back, half-lidded eyes, and the way she methodically ran her thumbs across each other were evidence that she longed for retreat. Nevertheless, good manners prevailed. An admirable trait. One of her many.

Before his admiration addled him completely, Gustaf turned his attention to Erwin. He supposed the man had redeeming qualities. But his clothing was a little too clean, and his hands not as rough as those of a farmer who worked the land. Raelene needed a hardworking man, not a fop.

"Yes, you may come on Tuesday, next week," Raelene said, startling Gustaf from his observation. She shifted from one foot to the other and schooled her expression, but he'd caught a flash of annoyance before she reined it in. She didn't like Erwin. Something in Gustaf's chest unknotted with relief. "Mr. Hanssen will be at the farm and can serve as chaperone."

Erwin failed to conceal his annoyance. Both overgrown eyebrows shot up as he glanced Gustaf's way. Gustaf swelled with an air of importance, making it clear that he was in charge. Surely the little wart didn't think he'd have access to the lady without a proper chaperone. It wasn't done.

"Of course," the man said, recovering with a bright smile. "Then I shall come midmorning."

Raelene dipped her head. "Very well." She started to step away. "I hope you have a pleasant week."

Erwin once again reached for Raelene's hand. "Anticipation at seeing you will improve my week tenfold."

With that, the prospective suitor departed, leaving Gustaf and Raelene standing face-to-face.

"Did I meet with your approval, sir?"

Her manner was as brittle as ice with formality. It wasn't his fault the marriage stipulation was in her father's will. But if he were in her place, he'd be angry, too.

"Miss Strattford, your manners were perfect," he told her, letting her misplaced hostility slide. With a "Humph!" Raelene whirled away, storming past a cluster of guests preparing to leave. As two women from the church stepped into her path to say their good-byes, her entire demeanor changed. A smile that would melt ice replaced the thin line of her lips.

Gustaf shook his head in exasperation. His was a hopeless situation. Somehow he'd get through this. With God's help, he'd fulfill his promise and be on his way.

৯

The day of planting arrived, and so did Erwin Murphy. Raelene had a direct view to the front of the barn where Gustaf paced back and forth like a military sentinel on guard duty. She didn't know why he seemed so concerned. It wasn't as if anything was happening.

With her hand in front of her mouth, she barely managed to conceal a yawn as she sat and listened to Erwin read several selections of poetry. She tried to remain focused on her guest, but her eyes strayed to the barn every time Gustaf appeared. Even at his most infuriating, he was more appealing than the educated Mr. Murphy. Her attention shot back to her present company.

Casting a glance around the farm, Raelene pictured little Erwins in her mind and inwardly shuddered. This had to stop. *Now.* She'd asked Gustaf to find her a husband, and he'd done his part. But she couldn't do hers. Not with Mr. Murphy, anyway.

Raelene cleared her throat, causing Erwin to pause. Relief coursed through her at the blessed silence. She hoped his verbal discourse was over. "Mr. Murphy, do accept my sincerest apology. But as you are no doubt aware, we are in the middle of planting preparations, and it is going to require as much assistance as can be gathered." A silent plea echoed in her mind that he wouldn't offer to help. "I do appreciate your taking time away from your farm to read to me some of your favorite poetry, but I'm afraid I cannot tarry any longer."

Disappointment clearly displayed on his face, Erwin closed his book in resignation and stood. "Say no more, Miss Strattford. I will take my leave immediately." Setting his hat on his head, he made his way to his wagon alongside the cottage. Propriety demanded that Raelene follow when she wanted to go inside and begin preparations for dinner. The neighbors coming to help with planting, as well as the workers they'd hired, would be famished by midday, and she could at least offer some refreshment.

"Thank you for your kind hospitality, Miss Strattford," Erwin said in a stilted but polite voice from his seat on the wagon bench. . .as though he recognized the futility of his visit. "May your farm see great success." With a tip of his hat, he drove off.

28

Gustaf studied the expanse of freshly cleared fields. His team had done its job for the initial pass. Raelene, a handful of their neighbors, and the hired help had done the rest with hoes, axes, billhooks, and digging sticks. Pride at what they had accomplished made him smile.

He snatched his hat from his head and bent to one knee as he raised his face toward the sky. "Father in heaven, You bless this humble work. Thank You for Your goodness." *If only You'd bless my task of finding a good husband for Raelene as much*, he added in silence.

A cat screeched, startling Gustaf from his prayer.

"By my troth, if I step on that cat's tail again, I will kick it to kingdom come!"

The frustrated voice coming from within the barn made

Gustaf chuckle. At least it wasn't anything serious.

"Gustaf, will we start close to the barn or at the far end and work our way back?" Jurien Layne stepped out from the barn with a hoe in hand and shaded his eyes from the sun that had turned his yellow hair a white gold. The son of Dutch and British parents, he bore the characteristic fair coloring of his heritage.

Gustaf stood and turned toward his best friend of more than ten years. Always there when needed and offering to help no matter what the chore. Jurien's hard work was balanced by his penchant for stirring up mischief at every opportunity. When he learned of the state of affairs at the Strattford farm, he'd volunteered to double his own workload.

"Working for the woman who refused you, despite having her father's blessing. That penance deserves special merit." Jurien studied Gustaf in a way that always made him uneasy. "Unless there is more to your personal sacrifice than simple charitable service."

Jurien also didn't miss a chance to put his own slant on the circumstances.

At Gustaf's prolonged hesitation, Jurien slapped his thigh and beamed a wide, gap-toothed grin. "I knew it! You still have a feather in your cap for her."

Rather than lie and deny it, Gustaf held his tongue. But given the distance Raelene was determined to keep between them, his true feelings meant nothing. "Jurien, I tell you the truth. Anything other than business is not possible."

Jurien shrugged. "Our Lord works in mysterious ways."

Although a man of faith, Gustaf had his doubts about any divine influence regarding Raelene. It would take a change of heart and soul for Raelene to look at him as more than a farm worker.

Motion alongside the cottage caught his attention. Raelene stood by the wagon as Erwin climbed up and bade farewell. As soon as Erwin was on his way, Raelene pivoted on her heel, gave Gustaf a hard glare, and disappeared. A moment later, the back door to the cottage slammed shut.

"You can see, my friend, there are no good feelings for me," Gustaf muttered.

"But even fewer for Mr. Murphy," Jurien observed. He winked. "Best we put our minds on things a man can make sense of, like farming." He pointed to the lane where another wagon passed the departing Mr. Murphy. "See? Benjamin and Gabriel have arrived. We have work to do."

On the wagon with Benjamin and Gabriel were their wives, Margaret and Anne, as well as Kaariana Janssen, whom Jurien had been courting. Upon reaching the wagon, Gustaf removed his hat, head dipping in a show of gratitude. "Thank you very much for coming today. You will be a great help in getting the land ready for planting. Raelene will be out soon. She had a visitor," he explained.

"A visitor?" one of the women asked with a lift of her brow.

"Competition for Gustaf," Jurien teased, giving Gustaf a jab in the ribs.

"I cannot say what Mr. Murphy is. I speak as the overseer, nothing more." Gustaf made a sweep with his arm encompassing the fields beyond the farmyard. "You can see," he said, changing the awkward subject, "that God Almighty blesses our work. If the weather stays good, we will have a generous crop."

Jurien handed him some seed and a hoe, a knowing twinkle in his gaze. Thankfully, his friend let the matter of Raelene pass.

"The land is ready to plant."

"That is why we've come today, good friend," Benjamin said, helping the women down from the wagon.

"You know about mounding. Ja?" At their nods, he continued. "We will do this today. The hired hands are already working in the other fields. Each of us will take a section in this field close to the house to work."

In no time at all, the men stood ready with their broad hoes, and the women had taken up digging sticks. While Gustaf divided the seed Raelene had purchased from Mr. Borgson into two pails for each couple, she emerged from the cabin in her work dress to join them.

"Did you enjoy your visit, Raelene?" Kaariana asked, her bright blue eyes sparkling with mischief. The young woman was the perfect match for Jurien, Gustaf mused, watching Raelene grow suddenly wary.

Avoiding Gustaf's attentive gaze, she replied, "Mr. Murphy is a fine gentleman who no doubt will make some woman a good husband."

"Some woman?" Kaariana pressed playfully.

"*Some* woman," Raelene answered, making it clear that *some* did not include her.

Gustaf suppressed the smile that threatened his lips as Raelene tied her apron securely behind her back.

"So, are we going to work this afternoon or not, Gustaf? Benjamin spoke up. "Where should Anne and I start?"

Gustaf tore his gaze from Raelene, a betraying heat creeping up his neck. "You and Gabriel work with your wives on the middle section." He turned in time to catch Jurien winking at Kaariana. Pink rushed to the maid's cheeks. "Jurien, you and Kaariana start near the chickens and work toward the large oak on the western end." Gustaf ventured a look at Raelene, whose humor was barbed at best. *Almighty God, please let this work.* "Raelene and I will take the area near the cottage."

"With eight of us working together, we should be finished before dusk." Gabriel stretched his brawny arms over his head, tightened the string holding back his charcoal black hair, and placed his left arm around his wife's waist. "What say we make a little wager?"

"Gabriel," Gustaf chided, "you know I do not make bets."

"Now, Gustaf, I do not mean with money," Gabriel reassured. "The team that finishes last has to make supper for the others." He patted his ample middle with his free hand. "And as the largest of this group, I can eat a fair amount."

"Then you had best make sure you are not last, or you and Anne will be in the kitchen a long time." Benjamin chuckled, taking up the challenge.

Margaret placed her hand on her husband's arm and smiled. "Benjamin, if you work as fast as you eat, we should be among the first finished."

"We are ready. Ja?" Gustaf announced, eager to escape the couples' companionship for the distraction of hard work.

With supplies in hand, they all headed for their designated areas. Gustaf hiked his hoe on his shoulder and headed toward the section he and Raelene were to work, aware that she fell in behind him, silent.

"The working arrangements are good, ja?" he said over his shoulder in a low voice. "You learned mounding only a few days ago when you add to your garden. But we will not plant squash today. We will plant corn and beans. I do not want you to feel badly around the other farm women."

"I am grateful for your thoughtfulness."

Her tone was cold. *Father, help me.*

He dug the hoe into the earth and piled the dirt into a mound. "I will do this in an even spread as we work down the rows." With the digging stick, he made two holes in the mound. Stepping toward the two tin pails of corn and beans he'd set down nearby, he reached into the one with corn and dropped a few kernels into the top indentation. "Corn will go in top. Beans will go at bottom." After sprinkling in the beans, he covered the holes with dirt.

"So, we will plant both into the same mound."

"Ja, the beans use the cornstalk as a pole to stay straight and tall. We will check later to stop the weeds from growing."

Raelene grabbed handfuls of each type of seed and placed them in two pockets on the front of her apron. It was ingenious. She'd obviously sewn them in preparation for today, because he'd never noticed such deep pockets in her apron before. The other women had no choice but to transport their pails with them as they moved along the rows.

She looked up in time to catch him watching her, dumbfounded. "What do you think?"

He cleared his throat. "Inventive," was all he could manage.

"If we are to make certain not to finish last, this will help our pace." For the first time that day, Raelene smiled.

Gustaf wanted to return the expression, but hesitated, lest he break the spell. Besides, she hadn't smiled for him but for her own creativity. No doubt, she was delighted at the chance not to have to cook for a change, but the moment the others were gone, the walls would go up again. He'd be left on the outside.

"Ja, good thinking," he said cautiously, determined not to tip her mood one way or the other. He moved ahead to dig the next mound. "But our work is not done with mounding and planting. We will have to come back to plant fish in each mound to fertilize. Then we keep the weeds away and watch as seeds take root and sprout."

Raelene dug into her pocket for more corn, but not before Gustaf saw the flash of disappointment in her eyes at his indifferent reply. She waited in pronounced silence until the mound was ready, then dug the holes and inserted the seeds as shown.

It is just as well, he thought. The less communication they had, the easier it would be to get lost in his work. But the longer the silence lasted, the more his conscience was pricked by guilt. Ignoring her misery to protect himself went against his grain. As a believer in God Almighty, his duty to minister to her superseded his personal feelings. *Father, help me find the right words.*

As she planted the mound he'd just made, an inspired thought entered his mind. "These seeds are like us," he began.

Confusion skimmed over her face.

"After we are born, we need care so when we are older, we will be productive. Our roots are formed from the instruction of our mother and father and other people in our lives."

He moved down the row, working as he spoke. A glance at his companion revealed piqued interest. "When we are ready, we break free from our family, like you divide your flowers when they grow too thick, and we become mature plants—independent, but from the same roots. If the conditions are right, we grow a strong foundation like our parents had and produce smaller plants to be separated when strong enough. And so the cycle goes, no?"

Raelene poked two holes in the resulting mound, exactly as he'd shown her. "I never thought of farming and family in that perspective."

"Our faith in God is almost the same way."

❧

Raelene dug into her apron, making a fist around a handful of beans. God *again*. She groaned inwardly. Why did Gustaf insist upon connecting the analogy to faith? It would have been fine to leave it as a parallel to their physical growth. She didn't want to hear anything about God or how much she needed Him. Her life couldn't be compared to seeds tended as they grow. God had uprooted her and left her to wither and die without water or sustenance.

Gustaf continued without looking up. "We begin as little seeds when we first believe. By reading the Bible and going to the parish with others who believe, we receive the nourishment to grow."

Raelene tried to ignore his words, but it was impossible not to hear them.

"We live and plant seeds in others and help them grow as we grow. If our faith is strong, when the rain and winds and storms come, we survive."

The winds and storms hadn't stopped since her parents' deaths, she fumed in rebellion. And she was surviving, but not by God's help. She'd had to compromise her own desires, use her own innovation. She was using Gustaf to save her parents' farm just as she'd promised she would. Although, she had to admit, she was enjoying his company far more than she thought she would, more than she wanted to.

And certainly far more than the boring Mr. Erwin Murphy. She had thought that man would never leave so that she could show Gustaf her new invention. Yet after the hours she'd spent reading her father's books on farming and discovering a way to make the work easier, he acted as if her ingenuity didn't matter a whit.

Raelene glanced at the progress of the others. She and Gustaf would finish far ahead of them, thanks to her. But instead of running on about her brilliance, he all but ignored it, rambling on about God and storms.

She remained quiet and focused on the planting. *Let him continue to talk to himself. Perhaps that audience will be preferable to my participation.*

But soon, Gustaf lapsed into silence, a silence that felt as cold as the April winds blowing through the trees at the northern edge of her farm. At least they agreed on something. Not talking would prevent disagreements or arguments. And since almost all of their conversations ended in some form of conflict, maybe silence was the answer.

nine

Gustaf reined in his horse and dismounted at the outskirts of New Castle. Handing the reins to the young lad waiting outside the town corral, he held out a coin.

"Treat her well, and you might see another upon my return."

The boy beamed a wide smile. "Yes, sir! She will receive the royal treatment."

He patted the lad's shoulder and strode off in the direction of the courthouse. Planting season had commandeered all of his spare time between working two farms. He missed the opportunity to converse with members of the assembly and other men in town on the latest happenings throughout the colonies. Being the second-born son had its advantages. With Stefan assuming the lion's share of the responsibility for the farm, Gustaf was free to pursue his interests in politics and events both local and abroad.

Although Raelene believed him to be nothing more than an uneducated farmer, at least in town he could embrace a lesser-known pastime. A lad was hawking the latest issue of the *Pennsylvania Gazette*. Gustaf signaled the boy to approach and gave him a few halfpence. After Benjamin Franklin had purchased the *Gazette*, it fast became the most successful newspaper in the colonies. Gustaf snapped open the paper and read the headings, wondering what news from Philadelphia or outrageous reports he'd find in this issue.

His favorite outlandish announcement was from last November. The postmaster, Benjamin Franklin, had published news of the wife of a peasant being brought to bed by the impending delivery of eight children, seven girls and a boy, all healthy and living. Gustaf couldn't fathom having two children at once, let alone eight. How the woman coped, he had no idea.

The first notice to catch his attention was an announcement of an expedition headed for the Spanish West Indies.

"Gustaf, your timing is impeccable." Jeremiah Shaw hailed him from the front steps and main doorway of the courthouse. "Planting season has no doubt kept you from town; am I right?"

From the dark cloak fastened with two buttons over his narrow frame to the tan breeches and dark stockings covered by buckled shoes, Jeremiah was the picture of dignified society in New Castle. The customary powdered wig was absent in rebellion of the British custom, and a single ribbon tied back his dark hair at the neck.

Gustaf ascended the wide steps and joined his friend, spying a copy of the same newspaper in his hand.

"Ja, and as overseer for the Strattford farm, I cannot come to town when I like. Have I missed much?"

With a reportedly weak constitution from frequent bouts of illness, Jeremiah wasn't suited to working a farm like Gustaf. But his connections to the assembly through his father had benefited Gustaf more than once.

Jeremiah held up the paper and pointed to an article at the top. "There has been a command from Governor George Thomas. He is commissioning as many as are willing to enlist to join the expedition for attacking and plundering the Spanish West Indies!"

"Ja, I was about to read that."

"Ironic, don't you think? We have had our own legislature and assembly here in New Castle for almost forty years, but we are forced to remain under Pennsylvania's jurisdiction."

"At least we are allowed to meet here in New Castle. Better than having all of our decisions taking place in Philadelphia, no?"

"True." Jeremiah's expression turned grim. "My older brother has been summoned, as have Abraham and Jacob Gooding, among others from Pennsylvania's three southern colonies."

"Both sons?" Gustaf felt like he'd suffered a solid blow to his midsection. He'd known the Gooding family since he was a boy. What would Josiah do with his only sons gone on some military expedition?

Jeremiah seemed to read Gustaf's thoughts. "Only one of the Curtis sons is called, so Samuel is going to send two of his other sons to help out on the Gooding farm."

"I wondered how Josiah would get through planting season without them. Samuel is a good man. I will tell Far and Stefan. They will help, too. I am busy with my farm and the Strattford farm. But I will help where I can."

Jeremiah folded the paper and tucked it under his arm, then gave his cloak a tug downward. "So I have heard, but I am interested in the news from your mouth. How are things faring with that irascible young maiden to whom you have indebted your service?"

Gustaf grew wary at the eagerness displayed on Jeremiah's face. He was as bad as a woman in a quilting circle sometimes. Gustaf chose his words carefully. "We get along well."

Jeremiah flashed a conspiratorial grin, the same one that had won him the favor of many a fair maiden. "Well, you say? I would venture a guess that you are still far more besotted by the fair-haired beauty than you care to admit." He threw his arm around Gustaf's shoulders and forced him to bow to Jeremiah's shorter stature. "Come, come. I know you had the good fortune to obtain a view of the land agreement her father signed."

Gustaf breathed a sigh of relief. Jeremiah hadn't taken up matchmaking after all. "Ja, and everything was good. Miss Strattford became the full owner when her father died."

"No clause of any kind that would provide you or anyone else with access?"

Gustaf hesitated. He'd been careful to speak only with

Jurien about the truth of his circumstances, but even he didn't know everything. Jeremiah was trustworthy. Of that, Gustaf had no doubt. And he needed to get this off his chest.

"Ja, there was one thing. Miss Strattford got very upset."

An interested gleam shone in Jeremiah's eyes.

"She must marry before her eighteenth birthday or she loses the land back to the assembly."

"And when is this fated day?"

Gustaf would no doubt regret this, but he'd come this far. No sense not sharing the complete details. "Fifteen, October."

"That's less than six months hence."

"Ja, I know the time is not long, but there is more. Miss Strattford and I argued about this. Now I must find a husband for her."

Jeremiah slapped his thigh with the newspaper and chortled. "I must say, that is the most humorous bit of information I have had the pleasure of being told in quite some time."

A sense of urgency rushed in at Jeremiah's raised voice. "You cannot tell anyone. The agreement must be honest. If men learn this, there could be problems. I want Miss Strattford safe." *As if I haven't done enough already.* "I promised to help, and I will not break that promise. No deceit."

Jeremiah held out his free hand without hesitation. "On my honor."

Gustaf clasped Jeremiah's hand in a firm grip. "Thank you." He placed his tricornered hat on his head and positioned it. "Now I have many shops to visit. Then I will return to the farm. Give my greetings to your father and brother. I pray he returns from his travels quickly and in good health."

Jeremiah gave his friend a two-finger salute in parting. "By your leave."

Relief filled him at bringing Jeremiah into his full confidence. Although he'd uttered many long petitions to Almighty God, having someone of flesh and blood made the task seem less daunting.

In no time at all, he'd completed his errands and returned across the cobblestone street to the corral. Under his arm, he carried a copy of the latest *Poor Richard's Almanack* for Raelene and a dusty volume of a novel written by Daniel Defoe entitled *Robinson Crusoe* that Mr. Walwoord from the dry goods store had recommended and sold him. If Raelene was going to continue reading to him during their midday meals, he wanted to choose some of the stories she read.

As he rounded the corner of the candle shop, he stopped fast upon hearing Raelene's name.

"Yes, the Strattford maid," Preston Sanbourne was saying. "I have it on excellent authority that she will be agreeable to what I have to offer. It has been my pleasure to observe her during her visits to town. The opportunity to turn that observance into a more permanent arrangement is one I simply cannot ignore."

Gustaf peered around the corner, careful to remain concealed from the small group of men assembled in front of the tavern. At the center was Sanbourne, a braggart if ever there was one. As the man revealed partial contents of the Strattford will, Gustaf's anger began to fester. Where had he learned that information? Surely not from Jeremiah! Sanbourne must have eavesdropped on their conversation. Guilt weighed heavily on his heart at his role in spreading Raelene's humiliating circumstances. Instead of protecting her, he'd made it worse. All because he wanted to share his burden. He should've left it with God.

Gustaf wanted to beat Sanbourne's words back into him, but violence was not the answer. It would only spread the news faster. Thankfully, Sanbourne wasn't sharing everything with his comrades, but he obviously knew enough to cause trouble.

Taking the path behind the tavern to the corral, Gustaf gave the lad another coin, mounted his horse, and pointed her toward home. The near-hour ride gave him ample time to formulate a plan.

☙

"Why can you not understand or respect my wishes, Mr. Hanssen?"

Gustaf remained with his back to Raelene, staring out the diamond-paned window at the rain that fell as she reprimanded him. Once again, he had tried to turn their discussion after the midday meal toward God and faith.

"You know nothing of what I have endured, nor can you comprehend all I have lost, beginning when Father moved us here from our home in England." She placed the marker in the newly acquired copy of *Robinson Crusoe* and placed the book in her lap. "We had it all—servants, fancy gowns, invitations to the most affluent of societal events, and the promise of aligning my family with another of equal or greater standing than our own."

The nerve of the man, she thought, running her fingers over the worn cover of the book. Her pleasure upon receiving this wonderful gift had been quickly dampened by Gustaf's desire to use Crusoe's rejection of his father's advice as a parallel to her own decision to turn her back on God.

"How can someone like you begin to imagine what that life is like? Farming is all you have known, and you still have your entire family with you."

If only he would allow her to read without interjecting his perspectives on the state of her relationship with God. The story of a lone English adventurer on the high seas could make their forced situation more than bearable.

When Gustaf finished drying the last of the dishes and turned to face her, a mix of sympathy and hurt dominated his face. Mouth downturned, he took a step forward then stopped, propping one leg on the bench at the table. Clearly at odds with himself, he folded his arms across his chest, then dropped them to his sides and at last clasped them in front of him.

The man made what she had always considered an ample kitchen seem much smaller. It was impossible to ignore him, even though warning bells rang at the prospect of giving him her full attention. Why couldn't he simply dispense with the platitudes so they could finish the chapter before they had to resume work for the afternoon?

She nervously opened the book again and made a show of trying to find her place, even though it was well marked. His silence was as bad as his penchant for preaching.

"Miss Strattford," he began after an interminable time, "I know you suffer." He paused and cleared his throat. "And I see your pain."

Raelene tapped her foot on the floor. He always cleared his throat to speak when they were alone. Did she make him as nervous as he made her? The idea wasn't entirely unappealing.

Squaring his shoulders, he folded his arms across his chest. "You are impatient like a wounded animal, because you are in pain. It hides the good and decent person inside and makes you swim in self-pity and anger at the only One who can heal you. But you should know, Miss Strattford. Your pain is nothing compared to what His Son suffered in your place." With a look that nailed Raelene to her chair, Gustaf straightened and marched for the door. Jerking it open, he slapped his hat on his head and paused. "Continue to blame Him if it is your wish, but it will not heal the hurt inside. You must give it to Him."

The door slammed behind Gustaf, leaving Raelene stunned. But the tearing at her insides would not be contained. She raised the back of her hand to her stinging eyes and wiped away a bitter tear. First one, then another. . .and another. Her anguish tore from her throat in a sob of hopelessness. *If only. . .* She hugged herself, starting to rock with the brutal onslaught. *If only what Gustaf said were that easy.*

❧

Gustaf ran the brush down Valdig's neck and across the gentle slope of his back, working out his frustration through the methodical routine. He'd already given Jägar a daily grooming, but the tension in his shoulders hadn't yet relaxed. How that woman could tweak the one nerve that invariably caused him to lash out without taking time to think before speaking!

Valdig sidestepped Gustaf's heavy-handedness and twisted his head around to nudge Gustaf's arm.

"I'm sorry, boy." He stroked the animal's forelock and resumed brushing at a gentler pace. Leave it to God to use one of His creations to send a simple message to him. Gustaf turned his eyes heavenward.

"Father above, You know how deep is Raelene's pain. I can only try to reason with her. Her heart is hard, and only You can make it soft. Please bring her back to You. Let me be like Your hand to offer comfort where I can. Use Your servant and take my humble offer."

Peace settled over him at leaving the situation in God's capable hands. He should know better. Every time he tried to handle things himself, he only succeeded in making them worse. Gustaf had planted the seeds, perhaps more of them than were needed. But only God could work the miracle Raelene needed to make them grow.

Later that night, as he carried some blankets up the ladder to make a bed in the hayloft of Raelene's barn—a decision he'd made after hearing Preston declare his intentions to pursue Raelene earlier that day—Gustaf wondered if he'd already gone too far.

ten

When he turned the situation over to God, Gustaf hadn't known it would still be so difficult to fulfill his promise. He had introduced three men to Raelene in the past month. And she'd found something wrong with each one. The woman was impossible to please.

If he were to admit the truth, so was he. Not a one had he really been comfortable in introducing to Raelene, despite having checked on their characters and abilities to take over in his stead once she was married. Sometimes he felt more like Raelene's father than a reluctant matchmaker, unwilling to show favor on any man because no one was good enough for her. And being forced to chaperone each meeting was sheer torture, even if it did give Gustaf insight into the lady's nature. He'd picked up on little nuances of disapproval that she tried to hide behind a facade of politeness.

Today, Nicholas Ridgely had chosen to call upon Raelene at noontime, effectively interrupting their daily routine. Long in the face and narrow at the shoulders, the man struck Gustaf as someone better suited to an educated profession than to hard labor, although he'd checked out the man's qualifications. Good family, educated, and serving as counsel to the assembly. He could hire an overseer if need be. Raelene invited Gustaf to join them for dinner, but he wasn't as good at hiding his true feelings as Raelene. Or worse, he'd say something foolish, demonstrating his lack of formal education.

So he declined. "I am behind in my chores, so I will work through the noon meal today." Gustaf had taken his plate and backed away as if fire nipped at his heels. A moment later, he backtracked and stood in front of them. "Thank you, Miss Strattford, for the venison and rice. I will bring back the trencher when I am done."

He piddled about close by like a watchdog, making a show of fixing one of the new stable doors that had swollen and needed its edge shaved. All he could see was the flash of panic that had entered her eyes when he had declined to join them. At least, he thought it was panic. For all his observation of Raelene, when it came to her feelings regarding him, she was a puzzle.

But she needed to make up her mind without his influence. That would never happen as long as he remained on hand and provided her with an excuse. He ran the carpenter's plane over the edge of the door, watching as a paper-thin layer of wood curled up behind the razor-sharp blade.

As Gustaf felt the smooth edge of the unfinished wood with his fingers, voices drew his attention to where Raelene had led Nicholas outside to sit beneath the shade of a tall oak. Had she done that to remain in his sight, or did she merely wish to enjoy the warmer weather of late spring? Gustaf set the door against the side of the barn to mount it on its hinges later and walked over to the woodpile. The constant need for split wood would allow him to remain nearby, if indeed she really felt more secure in his presence.

Despite the *whoosh* of the ax cutting through the air and the loud *crack* of the splitting wood, Nicholas's attempts to sustain a conversation still reached Gustaf's ear.

"You have done. . .a—a lot with this farm."

"Thank you. It has not been accomplished without a great deal of effort and the assistance of several workers."

"You are to be commended."

Raelene took a bite of the cookies she'd made for dessert and chewed with slow contemplation. "Tell me," she began after swallowing, "have you much experience working a farm?"

Nicholas reacted with so much enthusiasm, Gustaf thought he'd fall off the bench. He almost overturned his plate. "Oh my! Do forgive me." He wet his lips. "Yes. I have w–worked all my life on our farm. B–but in a lesser capacity than my father and brothers."

Great. If this nervous stammering continues, it will take Nicholas until this time next year before he communicates his interest. Nicholas was the first of Raelene's suitors for whom Gustaf actually felt sorry. It was a matter of time before Raelene sent him scampering like the rest, although she'd do it kindly.

"Mr. Ridgely, I do appreciate your taking the time to call on me and share our meal," she said. "Will you have another cookie?"

"Oh, n–no, thank you, Miss Strattford. It has been my pleasure." He was clearly smitten, devouring Raelene with his gaze as if she were the dessert.

She offered a patronizing smile as she folded her hands in her apron. "I apologize for my haste to end our visit, but as I am certain you are aware, harvesttime will be here before we know it. Much remains to be done, and I have many obligations to meet by harvest's end."

Nicholas made no attempt to conceal his disappointment, but he graciously stood and assisted Raelene to her feet. "I understand completely, miss, though I am stricken w–with regret." He offered a stiff bow, leg extended. Then they walked to the barn, where he clumsily mounted his horse. "I hope to call again s–soon."

"Perhaps when time permits, sir," Raelene responded with a gracious, if somewhat shallow, smile. As though mesmerized, she watched the man ride down the lane toward the main road.

Gustaf wedged the ax in the chopping block, waiting for Raelene to turn toward him or offer him one of the cookies. She didn't. Without warning, she gathered her petticoats in her hands and took off across the field instead. Before she was out of hearing range, a sob escaped her lips, tearing at Gustaf's heart.

Gustaf debated whether to follow her. So much had been thrust upon her young and delicate shoulders, and she'd borne it with grace. . .until now. As much as he wanted to run after her, perhaps she needed time to be alone.

Lord, be with her. The seemingly constant knot within his chest tightened as the prayer went up. *Help us both.*

❧

Raelene was breathless when she reached the orchard, her despair now nothing more than ragged gasps for air. What more would she have to endure before she lost her mind? As mannerly as Mr. Ridgely was, his stutter had been more than Raelene could handle. Her attention continually shifted toward Gustaf as he chopped the wood, admiring how he swung the ax with seemingly little effort. She couldn't help but compare Mr. Ridgely to Gustaf, and found Ridgely sorely lacking.

Once he departed, it was all she could do not to run to Gustaf in her exasperation, but she'd had to run somewhere. The orchard was one of her favorite refuges in times past, times when her distress paled in comparison to what she felt now.

Raelene's mind drifted back to when she and Mother had seen the variety of peach, cherry, and apple trees upon first purchasing the farm. They had been neglected and in need of restoration, a task with results that would make the toil worthwhile. The sweet scent of apples that had filled Raelene's nostrils had been the reason they'd chosen the area nearby to build.

With her knees to her chest and arms draped around her legs, Raelene dropped her head to her knees and sobbed beneath a cherry tree. She wanted to go back in time, back to childhood upsets, away from today's unbearable trial. The sound of a whinny from the fence adjacent to the orchard invaded her tortured thoughts. Raelene raised her head and wiped the tears from her eyes. Valdig. The horse had always been able to sense her mood. And he'd always been her confidant when she needed to talk out her dilemmas without censure, such as her longing for the life she'd left behind in England.

Valdig raised and dropped his head as if to say he remembered, too. It had been an extraneous expense to bring Valdig and Jägar with them on the ship, but Papa knew she couldn't bear to be away from them. He'd treasured his Jägar as much as she did Valdig. She'd fed them both treats of dried fruit and grain and spent a lot of days with them below deck—especially during storms. With a sniff, Raelene climbed to her feet and started toward the gelding.

"Oh, Valdig, remember when we lived in England? I took you for long rides through the countryside and dreamed of owning a small cottage on a simple estate. My cousins and I attended grand parties and delighted in all that English society has to offer." She spread her arms wide. "Now look at us. Left alone on this farm with no family and too far away from civilized noblemen and ladies for any social affairs to be remotely possible."

Stroking the white blaze between his eyes, she placed her other hand beneath his head and drew his face toward hers.

"A single person should not have to face this many hardships in less than a year."

"Maybe this trial has purpose."

Gustaf's words made her startle, which in turn startled the horse. Unlike Valdig, she did not recover her calm quickly, especially when the masculine scent of sweat, evidence of his hard labor, assailed her nose.

"Ingenting är så dålig så pass vi kan icke lära mycket av det," Gustaf quoted, his familiar accent that had once annoyed her now reminding her of Mother.

"Nothing is so bad that we cannot learn much from it."

Tears sprang to her eyes even as Father's words echoed in her mind: *"You must remain strong."*

Raelene sniffled, lamenting that she'd forgotten to put a handkerchief in her apron that morning. To her dismay, Gustaf produced a fresh one, although how he'd managed to keep it clean, she didn't know. Awkwardly, she accepted it, turning away in embarrassment as she dabbed at her eyes. A branch rustled behind her, followed by the snap of an early cherry being picked off the tree.

"Everything can look bad, but if you try to do the best with what you are given, the situation gets better."

She spun in challenge. "How—" To her frustration, she hiccuped with emotion. "How can you say something like that?"

"Because from big fights come big blessings." He held out the cherry in front of her. "This cherry tree suffers through wind, rain, snow, and ice. It has a time of winter with empty branches. But every year, it gives fruit."

Raelene took the cherry and rolled it back and forth in her palm. "I suppose you will now find some way to connect this analogy once more to God and tell me that He employs the world around me to show it's possible to persevere and prosper despite hardship."

He clenched his jaw. "If you would take your nose from air and look at the world where you live, you would see your great blessings." He turned in a half circle with arms spread wide, then stopped and faced her once again, his expression one of sorrow mixed with contempt. "But you judge all people you meet. You put them on one side of a scale with your life in England on the other side. That is a life you cannot have right now."

"*You* accuse me of being judgmental?" Raelene ranted. "If you would cease these attempts to force me into seeing life the way you do or having faith in God, who chooses to ignore heartfelt pleas, we wouldn't have to endure these worrisome confrontations." She pursed her lips as she beheld him from head to toe then back again. "But how could I expect you to understand?"

"Getting angry at me and others who help you, Raelene, will make you more unhappy. If you continue in your haughty ways, you will have no one left." He pivoted on his heel. "Good day!"

Raelene groaned as she watched Gustaf's retreat. What was it about the man that brought out the worst in her? It was just as well that her parents were not present to see what their daughter had become.

But he had insulted her just as much. Haughty ways, indeed. She wasn't haughty; she was frightened and desperate. If anyone should apologize, he should, for bullying her. The only way she'd apologize was if he did.

In the meantime, there were weeds to pull and fruit to gather. She'd promised baskets of cherries and future fruits to several women for pies and other treats. That was not haughty. That was being a good neighbor. The man was delusional.

❧

As dusk fell, Raelene stored the fruit baskets in the shade of the oak near the back door. She would deliver them tomorrow. As she started inside to retire for the evening, footsteps clumped on the dirt path between the house and the barn. Gustaf. Had he returned to deliver more insults?

"May I speak with you, Miss Strattford?"

At least the anger that had raged in his voice earlier was gone. Raelene watched him warily. "You have my complete attention, Mr. Hanssen."

Gustaf removed his felt hat and twisted it between his hands. "I apologize for my words this afternoon. I have been a bad example of a true believer in God Almighty." He avoided meeting her gaze as he continued. "I should show humility, but I show impatience and no control. I judged you, too. God forbid that be me."

Raelene shifted uneasily, recalling her vow not to apologize until Gustaf did. And now that he had...

"Mr. Hanssen, I—"

"You have a right to be angry with me," he said, cutting her off. "But I acted as I did because I care about you."

Raelene's heart fluttered.

"Your soul, I mean."

Then fell back in disappointment to its normal rhythm. But when Gustaf raised his head at her stunned silence, the sincerity in his eyes started the flutter once more. Before she could recover, he slapped on his hat and returned to the barn.

Shame found its voice, reminding her that she'd not apologized for her own rash words. Gustaf was right. She *did* compare everything and everyone in this horrid place to England. Raelene cast a guilty look at the barn and freshly planted fields beyond, a barn raised and fields planted by her neighbors. Common folk, but good people. People like Gustaf.

Gustaf was wrong, so wrong. Between the two of them, her actions and words had been far worse.

Raelene walked toward the barn. She would apologize. Not about her feelings toward God and Gustaf's insistence on browbeating her with his faith. But she would admit that she'd wronged him and her neighbors by comparing them to her English acquaintances. But for them, she and her promise to her parents would be lost.

eleven

June gave way to July, then August, and ushered in the highest heat of the summer. Raelene couldn't believe the height the corn had grown or the plentiful bounty of the beans.

It's actually happening! Mama and Papa's dreams are being realized.

She owed so much of the success to Gustaf. But every time he made her grateful for his help, he'd ruin it by mentioning God. The man and God were inseparable.

Raelene moved up and down the rows of mounds and jerked free the offending weeds wherever they tried to take root. It seemed like only yesterday when the stalks had brushed against her skirts. Now the crop towered over her. Never had she thought she'd feel this much pride in seeing the fruits of her labors from simple farming.

Gustaf had been right. Learning to farm *did* take a lot of time, and he'd been a patient teacher. Not that she deserved his patience. Even when he lost his temper because of something she said—and that seemed to be the only time he was able to reveal his true feelings—he always apologized, accepting full blame when it was not all his.

Raelene continued toward the wheat and ran her hands over the soft grains. They tickled her skin, making her feel so lighthearted, a giggle burst forth. She immediately covered her mouth as she sought out Gustaf, who was too far away to have noticed. What would he think if he saw her now? Like a child, she wanted to run through the fields, tossing her cares to the wind. She hadn't felt this good in months.

Gustaf's words interrupted her thoughts: *"If you would take your nose from the air and look at the world in which you live, you would see your great blessings."*

Those weren't his exact words, but the truth in them remained. She *had* been taking this farm and her privileged life in England for granted. Working with Mama hadn't been this difficult or exhausting, nor was it quite as rewarding.

"Do you walk alone, or can I come, too?"

Raelene started at Kaariana's voice and squealed as she ran to embrace her friend. It seemed like months since the young woman had visited.

"How long have you been standing there? And what brings you out this way? Is everything all right with your family?"

Kaariana placed both hands on Raelene's arms. "Everything is good. I come here to see you and see Mr. Hanssen. So I talk with him. Now I talk with you. And I have exciting news."

Her stilted speech betrayed her heritage. Kaariana's family had been among the first Dutch settlers of this area, and while their accent had faded somewhat, their speech patterns had not. Life had not been easy for Kaariana or her kin. But today, light shone from her eyes, and a glow not caused by the sun made her cheeks a rosy pink.

"Please do not force me to wait another second. I rarely receive a letter from my cousins in England, and the farm has kept me so busy, it's been more than a month since I've been to town. News would be quite welcome."

"I wonder why I not see you." Kaariana spun in a circle, her impish face raised to the sky. "We had such fun counting number of times Reverend Dalton would push back his wig from his excited preaching."

Frustrated by the obvious delay, Raelene stomped a foot and crossed her arms. "You're being absolutely merciless."

Kaariana quirked an eyebrow. "Oh! You wish to hear my good news, no?"

"As if there is any doubt."

Her friend leaned forward, and Raelene mirrored the pose.

"Jurien come to call yesterday afternoon, and my father say we can marry!"

Raelene straightened so fast, she nearly knocked heads with Kaariana. "Oh, that is wonderful!"

"He finally has a home for us and not want to wait. We will be wed on Sunday. Say you will come."

Sunday. That meant she would be obliged to also attend service at the town parish. Then the wedding. Would she be able to bear being in God's house for that long?

"You have bad thoughts? There is frown on your face."

The concern lacing Kaariana's questions gave Raelene pause. She had almost snuffed out her friend's happiness with her selfishness. How could she not attend the wedding of a friend who'd cheered her on more than one visit, not to mention helped shoulder some of the farm work?

Trying to grab hold of the joy she'd felt moments before, Raelene clasped her friend's hands. "Forgive me. I allowed my thoughts to drift toward an unpleasantness." She hoped her eyes didn't betray her inner struggle. "Of course I'll come celebrate with you. Nothing would please me more."

Kaariana embraced her again. "Wonderful." She wrapped an arm loosely at Raelene's waist. "Now, we go back to the house for celebration dinner. The handsome Gustaf will join us, no?"

Handsome is right, even if he is stubborn as a mule. But Raelene caught the teasing note in her friend's voice and feigned disinterest. "Yes, we share almost every midday meal together."

"The people in town, they say many gentlemen have come to call here."

How much should she reveal? Gustaf had been very discreet when he had invited the gentlemen to the farm. Could she trust Kaariana with the truth? No. Better to be indifferent.

"They no doubt have heard about my inheritance and see an unmarried woman with land as the opportunity to improve their social standing." She released a derisive snort.

"Not one of them has seemed to comprehend or be interested in all that's involved in running a farm. If they only knew."

"What do you mean?"

Raelene led the way inside and immediately set to work preparing the meal. "At one time, I was just like them. When we owned the candle shop and provided candles and scented soap to those who needed them, I believed we would remain there and continue to enjoy the convenience of living in town."

Kaariana worked alongside her. "And you were happy?"

"I thought I was." She sliced the beef Gustaf had provided and dumped it into the pot along with the vegetables. "The duties at the candle shop didn't require nearly as much energy, although the process was time consuming." She carefully hung the pot on the hook over the fire for the stew to cook.

While Kaariana prepared the custard, Raelene sliced the bread. "Here, I rise with the sun to gather the eggs, milk the cow, and put bread in the oven to bake. I usually break the fast alone, but on the occasional morning when Gustaf gets an early start, I have to prepare johnnycakes. Then there are vegetables and fruit to gather and some of the spices from the garden out back. Back home in England, servants did all of that."

"But you enjoy this work, no?"

"Yes, and that is what makes me realize any gentleman who wishes to be a part of this farm must also demonstrate a willingness and ability to work it."

"You do not wish to have servants?"

"As the farm grows, yes." After placing butter on the plate next to the bread, Raelene stirred the stew. "But Gustaf and I have proven the daily chores can be completed without extra people underfoot."

"My Jurien say you will not find one who works as hard as Gustaf."

"Hello again, Kaariana." Gustaf entered through the back door. Drops of water on his face and hands gave evidence of his recent washing. How much had he overheard? The door had not been firmly shut.

Raelene couldn't tell if her nervousness came from what he might have overheard or the fact that his masculine presence seemed to fill the room. It never failed to set her nerves atwittering.

"I hope you do not mind," Kaariana said. "I join you for dinner."

"It is good with me. But I think outside is better. The breeze is cooler than in the kitchen. If Raelene agrees."

Why would I mind? The midday meals weren't a private meeting. Raelene ladled out three steaming bowls of stew and placed them on her mother's tray. Gustaf's hands brushed hers as he took the tray and led the way to the bench beneath the oak tree.

⁂

"Kaariana, will you stay to hear the story of Robinson Crusoe?"

Gustaf had tucked the book under his arm on his way outside. He hoped Raelene would read this afternoon, despite the guest at their meal. Kaariana's face registered surprise at his invitation.

"A story?"

"Ja, Raelene and I enjoy reading after our midday meal. She has many books." He directed a teasing grin at Raelene. "*Robinson Crusoe* was a compromise."

Raelene tucked a strand of hair behind her ear and pressed her lips together. Her flushed cheeks never failed to warm him, as well. Without acknowledging him, she faced Kaariana with a composed demeanor. But Gustaf knew she was ill at ease by the way she worried the embroidered edges of her apron.

"Yes, Gustaf expressed interest in the reading material I had available," she explained. "So I agreed to share various selections as he cleared away our dishes."

Kaariana's eyes widened. "You do not clean? A man should work in field, no?"

Before Raelene could get defensive, Gustaf rushed to smooth over the misconception. "I have two sisters, but Mor always makes sure we help her with chores other women in the family would do if they were here." He leaned back against the trunk of the tree and crossed his one ankle over the other. "But I do not mind the chore, especially if it means I am treated to stories of faraway lands and adventures."

Kaariana shifted to her knees and sat back on her heels, an excited gleam in her eyes. "I have heard of this Robinson Crusoe. He travels on boat and finds trouble."

"Yes, but that is not all that takes place in the story." Raelene took the book from Gustaf. She opened it to the page she had marked when they had left off yesterday.

Father, please let her share the deeper, spiritual journey on which Robinson embarks. Let her see there is more to this story than the adventures, Gustaf prayed.

"We already read about how Crusoe's vessel was captured by Turkish pirates, how he established a successful sugar plantation in Brazil, and how he became a slave trader. But several hurricanes wrecked his ship on one journey and landed him on a desolate island."

A slight breeze stirred the loose tendrils of her hair and sent Raelene's lavender-soap scent toward Gustaf as she continued to summarize the story for Kaariana. He closed his eyes as the scent of her wafted his way, inhaling it, savoring it. . . .

What am I doing? Distance, he told himself sternly. He needed distance. There was no room for any sort of awareness beyond that of their business arrangement. He couldn't allow it. His pride had been damaged enough by her continual inference that he would never compare to her English cousins. He dared not put his heart at risk as well.

"Almost five years later, the English adventurer is still alone on this island. But he has found many ways to make life easier for himself and survive with what the island provides. He's started with nothing more than the few things washed ashore from the shipwreck and built himself a home with many comforts."

English adventurer. Gustaf latched onto those two words. Must be why she seemed to enjoy this story more than the others. It reminded her of England and Gustaf of the indisputable differences between her past life and his.

The realization overwhelmed Gustaf like a dark cloud. Yet he continued to listen in the hope that Raelene might recognize the similarities between her situation and Crusoe's. He, too, had lost everything but, despite overwhelming odds, had prospered. That same survival spirit existed in Raelene. If only she'd rely on it more.

"He survived alone for five years?" Kaariana asked.

Raelene tucked her ankles together at a ladylike slant. Even in the fields, she carried herself with grace.

"Yes," she replied. "But by now, he's built a home and become quite resourceful."

"Did he not have anger at God for what happened?" her friend pressed on.

Gustaf's pulse checked as he waited for Raelene's answer.

Raelene pursed her lips, nearly distracting Gustaf from her carefully composed answer.

"At first, yes. Memories of his father and the advice given made him pray and read the Bible daily. Although he'd initially scorned his father's words, through his bleak circumstances, he realized how true those words were and how much he needed God." Raelene fingered the pages of the book, suddenly contemplative.

Had she heard her own words? Gustaf found himself clenching his thigh in anticipation. Was her heart open to listening?

Her expression broke with a sudden brightness. "Would you like to remain while I continue reading?"

Gustaf's heart fell. If she'd seen any similarity in Crusoe's plight and her own, she'd dismissed it. Never in his life had he seen such a hardheaded woman.

"Yes," Kaariana exclaimed. "I wish to hear more of Mr. Crusoe. A very interesting story, this is."

Seemingly satisfied to have the attention of both listeners, Raelene resumed the story and read of how Crusoe remained on the island for another twenty-four years.

Please, Father. Let her heart absorb the deeper meaning. She will not be truly happy until she surrenders her anger.

Gustaf realized that no good could come of his growing attraction for the troubled young woman, but he wanted more than anything for her to turn back to God.

It was a hope he would not relinquish, at least until his promise to her father was fulfilled. If she'd not turned to God by the time Gustaf found her a husband, then the responsibility would fall to that man. Only then could Gustaf leave in peace. Until that time, neither of them would experience peace, short of a miracle.

twelve

Although September was upon them, Raelene still couldn't dislodge the memories of that afternoon. Passages of Robinson Crusoe's story floated across her mind. His triumphs and his failures. His good fortune and his great losses. Through it all, his faith and reliance on God remained unshaken. Just like Mama's and Papa's. Their faith had sustained them both in dark and happy times, and they'd raised her with it.

She remembered sitting on the floor at Papa's knees as he read scriptures and Mama sang. Even when Papa ended his commission in the British navy, knowing he would inherit next to nothing as the second-born son, her family hadn't complained. He wanted more than a lifetime of service to the king, and they followed.

How had she lost the faith and peace they'd shared?

Since that day she'd shared the meal with Kaariana and Gustaf, sleep had been difficult at best. In her dreams, she saw Mama and Papa together, smiling, reaching out for her. But then she saw their tears. And when she awoke, no matter how hard she tried, she couldn't figure out why they were sad.

She'd done everything they'd asked. She'd worked side by side with Mama in the candle shop, even when she wished daily to return to her grandfather's country estate and be with her cousins. When they purchased the farm, Mama had continued to teach her about cooking and cleaning and daily chores. Papa had also taught her a little about farming, and what he'd not taught her, he'd left to her in his books.

Unable to sleep, Raelene lay on her back staring up at the thatched roof. It hadn't been easy moving down to her parent's bedchamber, but the unbearable heat of the loft had left her little choice. At least the soft rhythm of the falling rain from the summer storm offered a reprieve from the high temperatures and soothed her troubled mind some.

"Maybe that is why I am seeing them in my dreams now," she muttered aloud. Being in this room where they had slept made her feel closer to them. But in her dreams, any comfort she might have was overpowered by the sadness Raelene saw in her parents' faces.

Was it because she had turned away from God? Didn't they understand how much God had taken away? Didn't they know she couldn't accept the pain He had allowed into her life? They were together. They were happy and together, not abandoned to face the cruel reality their deaths had created.

She could no more be like them than she could be like Robinson Crusoe. Shipwrecked with only the clothes on his back, he hadn't had the support of friends or neighbors. He hadn't even had a home. Yet he still acknowledged God's favor and blessings and read daily from the Bible. For twenty-four years, he praised and thanked God in the midst of his trials.

She'd at least had the support of friends—godly people— but her heart would not soften toward God. It rebelled against her longing to fill its emptiness with peace.

"Why can't I do that?" Raelene brushed away an errant tear. "I want that peace so badly."

A bright flash of lightning, followed by an immediate crash of thunder, made Raelene nearly jump out of bed. She fought to catch her breath and still her rapidly beating heart. Tossing the light covering aside, she arose and padded across the wood floor to the diamond-paned window.

As the storm intensified, she watched the progression of the natural waltz play out before her. Lightning danced in the dark clouds, filling the air with sparks and briefly lighting up the ominous swirls in the sky. Thunder answered in rumbling response. The rain poured down in opaque gray sheets against the blackened sky, almost obscuring the view of the fields behind the house. Raelene pushed open the window and breathed in the fresh scent carried on the storm winds. She extended her arm and allowed the cool rainwater to form rivulets on her skin.

A minute later, the drops hardened, stinging her hand. The clatter on the windowsill sounded like the pelting of tiny pebbles against metal, replacing the soft sound of the rain.

Hail!

Raelene froze. "Oh, no! The crops!"

In seconds, she threw a wrap around her nightdress and dashed outside toward the fields. A she stumbled blindly, loose strands of her waist-length hair whipped about her face, making it even more impossible to see where she was going. When she finally reached the edge of the first field, she fell to her knees in the muddy puddles.

"Look at the plants and see how they are faring!"

Gustaf's shout from at least two or three rows away startled her almost more than the initial thunderclap had. How long had he been there? And why wasn't he tending to his own crops? Raelene brushed aside her questions. That wasn't important now. The crops were, and she was grateful for his presence. *I would have been at a complete loss as to what to do.* Once again, he was putting the needs of her farm above his own.

Side by side, they moved up and down the rows of vegetables, then made their way through the wheat. Despite the ferocity of the storm, the diminutive pieces of ice weren't large enough to do much damage to the hearty crops. By the time they'd finished inspecting each row, the storm had receded and the downpour softened. Soaked to the skin in seconds, with mud seeping through the thin layers of her night shift, Raelene shivered and folded her arms to ward off the chill.

Gustaf whipped off his cloak and wrapped it around her,

tucking it beneath her chin. With his face so close, she had nowhere else to look, and neither did he. Lightning flashed, illuminating his face. The immediate warmth of his eyes and his cloak offset the damp chill. A tingle rivaling that from the lightning bolts surged through her. She breathed in his familiar scent that even the rain couldn't diminish. Gently, he freed her braided hair and loosened strands from underneath the cloak, never once breaking their visual connection.

After what seemed an eternity between heartbeats, he blinked. Then he cupped his hands around her elbows and pulled her to a standing position to escort her toward the cottage. In no time at all, Gustaf had the fire stoked and blazing and pressed a hot cup of tea into her hands, taking one for himself as they sat together in front of the hearth.

"Th–thank you," she stammered over the rim of the tin cup.

"It is my duty," he replied.

His duty, Raelene thought. But it was more than that. She knew it, and so did he. Why was he trying to downplay the importance of his presence here tonight? He seemed no more willing to admit that than he was to acknowledge the brief bond they'd shared while standing in the fields. He was trying so hard to maintain his distance. Had she really been that cold and reserved?

Yet despite her less-than-cordial treatment of him, here he was, enduring a summer hailstorm to make sure her crops remained safe and seeing to her comforts, as well. He could have stayed and helped his family, but he chose to help her instead. And for what? Land that he'd never own and crops that would bring profit only to her.

As they sat in companionable silence, allowing the heat from the fire to dry their clothes and warm their skin, Raelene realized just how cruel she'd been. Well, not anymore!

He'd borne her bitterness, biased assumptions, and unfair judgment with humility and patience. Even when he lost his temper and stormed off, he always returned to apologize and set things right. She'd given him nothing but hostility in return.

I've changed. And I'll prove it.

❦

Sunlight filtered through the window and fell on Raelene's face the next morning. Moaning, she rolled over and pulled the covers over her head.

The sun!

A new day had dawned and she had overslept. She dragged herself out of the warm cocoon of her bed. Her entire body ached, and her mind was so foggy from lack of sleep, she didn't know how she'd make it through the day. She had a vague memory of muttering "Good night" to Gustaf before stumbling to her bedchamber, but that was about it.

The tinny *clang* of a tool against what sounded like iron drew her to the kitchen door. Upon opening it, she spied Gustaf outside, pounding what appeared to be a horseshoe. As she watched, he returned it to the fire and then put it back on the anvil to hammer again.

Leaving the door open, she turned toward the fireplace and nearly tripped over the feather tick from her bed in the loft.

"Now how did that get here?"

Had Gustaf slept in the kitchen after she left? Raelene reached for the pillow on the tick and hugged it to her chest. She closed her eyes and breathed in the masculine scent as she recalled sitting in front of the fireplace with him just a few hours before.

"What am I doing?" She dropped the pillow. There was no time for fanciful daydreaming. The eggs needed to be gathered and the cows milked, and since Gustaf was already here working, she would whip up batter for johnnycakes.

Raelene dressed and reached for the pail before heading to the barn, nearly spilling the milk in it. Why, it was half full already! A glance in the basket sitting on the table confirmed the eggs had been collected, as well. How in the world had she not heard Gustaf this morning?

"I must have been more exhausted than I realized."

She stepped toward the back door. "Gustaf," she called out, hoping he'd hear her above his pounding. He stopped the hammer in midstroke and looked up. "Thank you for gathering the eggs and milking the cow this morning. I can prepare a meal for us if you wish."

"You are welcome," he called back. "And thank you, but I ate leftover bread this morning. It was enough."

When he returned to his work, Raelene realized she needed to get moving, as well. She made do with what was left of the bread and headed to her chores.

ॐ

As midday approached, Raelene stood outside, beating the rugs from the kitchen, bedchamber, and loft. She'd spent a few hours tending the garden while Gustaf repaired the damage to the thatched roof. Papa had secured a double layer and spoken of his plan to replace the thatch with wood. Perhaps that could be done before the harvest.

Once the rugs were back on the freshly swept floors, Raelene returned to the laundry. The *clop* of horse hooves on dirt drew her attention to the lane leading to the main road at the edge of her farm. She shielded her eyes from the sun, trying to identify the lone rider as he drew near.

He exudes a certain air of confidence, she thought as the man dismounted. His well-styled flaxen hair and pressed clothing bespoke a man of status. Or at least that he took pains with his appearance. When he caught sight of her, he swept his cocked hat from his head and bowed.

"Miss Strattford, I presume?"

She dried her hands on her apron and dipped a slight curtsy. "Yes, and who might you be?"

Tucking his hat under his arm and holding the reins to his fine steed, he smirked in condescension, as though she should have known his identity. "My name is John Singleton.

Perhaps you have heard of my family's substantial acreage north of town?"

Raelene bit back the sarcastic retort that came to mind and forced a polite smile to her lips. "Yes, I do believe your family paid mine a visit once or twice when we owned the candle shop in town."

His chest puffed proud as a peacock at her recollection. "That we did. But I do not recall a beauty such as yourself gracing that fine establishment."

From the corner of her eye, she noted Gustaf's slow approach, farm tools in hand and a scowl on his face. If she didn't know better, she might think he was attempting to look threatening. With effort, she remained focused on Mr. Singleton, but she couldn't resist a slight affront to his arrogance.

"Perhaps because I was only fourteen at the time and most likely below your line of vision," she replied pointedly.

Gustaf covered his mouth with his hand, an act Raelene suspected was to cover a laugh, and turned away. With effort, she maintained her composure as she waited for the remark to penetrate Mr. Singleton's pride. But when he realized what she'd said, to his credit, he showed minimal reaction to her barb, save a narrowing of his gaze.

"Yes, well, had I the fortune of making your acquaintance then, this meeting today might not be necessary."

Oh, please. Save me from this pretentious and self-absorbed boor.

"Miss Strattford!" Gustaf bellowed. "I am going into town to learn of the damage from the storm. If you wish to come with me. . ."

"Yes!" she answered a little too quickly. *Thank you, Gustaf.* Anything to get away from Mr. Singleton. Gustaf's company was far preferable.

Mr. Singleton cocked an eyebrow, appraising Gustaf from head to toe. The disdain in the visitor's expression rankled Raelene, but Gustaf met his gaze directly.

"And are you one of Miss Strattford's hired hands?"

Gustaf tightened his large hand around the handle of the mallet he'd used to shape the horseshoe and clenched his teeth. "I am the overseer."

"Well, would you be a good fellow and fetch some water for my horse?"

The sinew of Gustaf's arm flexed, a sure sign of his growing irritation.

Raelene rushed to intervene. "Actually, Mr. Singleton, I do apologize. But I am in need of supplies in town, and as Mr. Hanssen has so kindly offered to escort me, I must prepare for the journey. I pray you will forgive me for not being able to invite you to stay longer?"

The gentleman once again, Singleton bowed. "Of course, Miss Strattford. I would not wish to interrupt your plans. It was I who arrived unannounced." He settled his hat over his coiffed hair. "Might I call at another time, perhaps one that is more convenient?"

"We shall see."

"For your horse," Gustaf spoke up, "the trough by the barn is full. He can drink his fill before you leave. I will show you on my way to hitch the wagon."

"That will not be necessary, sir," Singleton announced stiffly, mounting the steed. "Good day, Miss Strattford." With a tip of his hat, he rode off.

As Gustaf cleared the farmyard, Raelene thanked him for intervening, earning a sheepish "My pleasure!" in return.

Blood rushed to her face. "I'll fetch my reticule and coins," she managed to say through the sudden dryness in her throat. With yet another unwanted suitor successfully discouraged, the day promised to be most pleasant after all.

❧

The storm had cut a wide swath of selective damage across the withered fields. Farther north, larger hail had fallen, piercing holes in barn roofs. But from all reports, everyone seemed to have fared well. Raelene and Gustaf had spent the better part of the past two hours speaking with many of their neighbors who had also come to town to purchase supplies or materials for repairs.

"Excuse me, Miss Strattford." Gustaf's hand pressing at Raelene's elbow sent heat rushing up her arm. "Jeremiah Shaw speaks with his father by the church, and I wish to hear him. I will return in a few moments."

Flustered, she replied, "Fine. M—meanwhile, I should like to visit the c—candle shop and replace the. . .the candles Mama favored so much." His proximity and touch made it difficult to think clearly. Raelene stepped a couple of inches away, but he didn't seem to notice. "Until I can arrange for a place to dry larger candles like the ones Mama and I used to make, I will have to purchase them."

Gustaf pondered her statement as though stymied by it. At length, he nodded, shaking off whatever distracted him. "I will come to the candle shop afterward," he promised.

After walking between the courthouse and the town green across from the church, Raelene headed for the shops lining the main street. The cobblestone streets fairly teemed with farmers, overseers, indentured servants, members of the assembly, and the resident townsfolk alike. So many different people from various stations in life, yet all coming together for a unified purpose. The sight reminded Raelene of the times she and her parents had walked these same streets when they lived in town. It also brought to mind the little country town in England near her grandfather's estate. How she'd loved to walk the cobblestone streets there or sit on a stone bench along the sidewalk and watch the hustle and bustle.

If she closed her eyes, Raelene could still smell the sweet honeysuckle at the edge of town and hear the birds chirping from the trees in the town square. She could almost taste the fresh bread the cheerful Miss Penelope always offered to

Raelene when she stopped by for a visit. Life was so different. She'd been raised with all the privileges afforded to a military family who had sworn allegiance to the Crown and been sheltered from the harsh realities of a farmer's existence.

Until now.

How much she'd taken for granted back then, she thought as she selected several special candles. The real trials of a farmer's existence, she now knew firsthand. Thus far, this season showed promise, unlike the recent past when, according to her neighbors, earthquakes and locusts had devastated the area. As much as the colonists had battled the elements, they deserved a good crop this year. And not only because it would mean good things for her, but because she'd come to respect—no, care—for her neighbors and fellow farmers since walking in their shoes. She truly wished for their prosperity as much as her own.

After exchanging pleasantries with the current owner and thanking him for his condolences regarding her loss, Raelene made her purchase. Her mind going a dozen directions at once, she stepped back through the open doorway and off the stone step into a ruffled, although solid, wall of man with a startled "Oomph!"

Her reticule and brown package sailed from her hands to the ground.

"My sincerest apologies, madame!" he gasped, equally surprised.

As Raelene bent to retrieve her personal belongings, the gentleman stayed her with a gold-ringed hand. "Allow me, please."

Still shaken, Raelene took note of his finely manicured nails with which he retrieved and wiped off her package and reticule. *This is a gentleman,* she thought, admiring the tailored fit of his doublet with its substantial turnbacks, ornate cuffs, and polished buttons. Unfastened, they revealed the ruffled shirtwaist into which she'd smashed her nose. The shirtwaist was tucked into coffee-colored breeches, above black stockings that disappeared into shiny shoes with polished buckles.

Flashing a most disarming smile, he bowed gracefully and handed her the items. "Do forgive me, Miss. . . ," he said, tipping a cocked hat upturned to perfection.

"S—Strafford," she supplied, so astonished by his impeccable manners that she nearly forgot her own name. Recognition dawned on his handsome face, lighting up eyes nearly as black as his hair and making his high cheekbones more pronounced. The result of excellent lineage, no doubt.

"Ah, yes. Strattford. Previous residents of this town, I believe, and prior owners of the establishment from which you just emerged. Am I correct?"

He knew too much to be a stranger, but how had she never had the good fortune to meet such a man before today? "Yes, that is correct." She released a nervous giggle, feeling utterly dowdy in her cotton dress and lappet cap in his pressed and polished presence. Reaching into her reticule, she withdrew her fan and snapped it open in front of her face in an attempt to recover some level of decorum. "Forgive me, sir. You appear to be familiar with my identity, but you have yet to introduce yourself."

"Preston Sanbourne, Miss Strattford. Please do accept my apologies for my lapse in manners."

Lapse? He'd been nothing short of flawless in his entire demeanor. His commanding presence and self-assured air differed from the pompous gentleman from whom she'd escaped earlier that day. Preston seemed every bit the country gentleman that her esteemed cousins had been back home, and similar to the ones she'd encountered when her family lived in town.

Preston. That she'd thought of him by his given name gave Raelene cause to stumble in shock.

Mr. Sanbourne placed a hand at her elbow to steady her.

"I hope you are not ill, Miss Strattford." Concern claiming

his aristocratic features, he gently led her to a shady area beneath a tall oak. "It is no doubt the heat of the day that has taxed you. Do rest a bit."

Leaning back against the tree, Raelene waved the fan in front of her face and brandished a sweet smile at her companion. Just as quickly as it formed, it faltered. Over Preston's shoulder, she saw Gustaf approaching from the church with a brooding countenance that made her heart jump.

Had he received bad news from Mr. Shaw? She tried to catch his eye, but he didn't appear to notice her. His attention was focused on Preston. The unconcealed contempt in his eyes could have wilted a flower. Could he possibly know something untoward about Mr. Sanbourne that she did not? She prayed not.

Gustaf looked in her direction, clearly struggling to soften his expression. He failed utterly.

"Miss Strattford," he said between clenched teeth, causing Preston to turn around in surprise. "If you are ready, the horses are rested. We can return to the farm." He extended his hand and silently invited her to step toward him.

"Good day, sir," Preston spoke up, offering his hand. "Preston Sanbourne, at your service."

Usually cordial and kindhearted, Gustaf stared sullenly at Sanbourne's extended hand as though it were leprous. This sort of oafish behavior had been welcome with the likes of their earlier visitor, but not with someone like Preston Sanbourne.

Raelene snapped her fan closed against her palm, eager to make amends. "Mr. Sanbourne, please forgive me. I fear our little collision has addled my wits. Allow me to introduce my overseer, Mr. Gustaf Hanssen. His family owns the farm neighboring my own."

"Mr. Hanssen," Preston repeated, extending his hand once more, a trace of smugness in his tone.

To Raelene's embarrassment, Gustaf hesitated a fraction

of a second before accepting the handshake, long enough for Raelene to know he did it only out of deference to her. "Mr. Sanbourne," he said, insinuating himself between Raelene and the gentleman as if drawing boundaries. And he was marking her clearly off limits.

Men!

Raelene stepped around Gustaf, eager to get away before he made a further buffoon of himself. "It was a pleasure to make your acquaintance, Mr. Sanbourne. Perhaps we shall meet again sometime." She handed Gustaf the package as he reached for her arm.

"I'm ready to return to the farm, Mr. Hanssen," she announced, gathering her purse to her waist and stepping away.

"Perhaps you will be attending services on Sunday?" Preston called after her. "And might I presume even the wedding immediately following?"

Delight washed over Raelene as she turned to answer. "Why, yes. Kaariana is one of my dearest friends. I would not miss it."

Mr. Sanbourne touched his thumb and forefinger to the front corner of his hat and bowed again. "Then I shall see you Sunday. It was a pleasure to meet you both. Good day."

It wasn't until Preston stepped inside the candle shop that Raelene realized Gustaf had left her in the middle of the street and was walking toward the buggy as though hounds nipped at his heels. Gathering her petticoats with her free hand, she rushed after him.

"And just what was the meaning of that ill-mannered exchange?" she exclaimed, breathless upon catching up with him.

He slowed but didn't stop. "I do not want to talk about it. You would not understand."

"I wouldn't—"

"Miss Strattford, please." He spun around to face her. "Trust me." With that, he whirled again toward the buggy.

Trust him? How could she trust someone she didn't

understand. . .especially after he had behaved in such an oafish manner? He wouldn't even give her the courtesy of explaining his actions. But why would he—?

A single answer entered her mind. No, that wasn't possible. Raelene tried to match his stride, her thoughts staggering as fast as her heartbeat. Could he have been jealous? Upset at Mr. Sanbourne's attention? He hadn't acted anywhere near as badly toward any of the other men who had come to visit the farm or introduce themselves. Why Preston?

Only last night, Raelene had begun to see Gustaf in a new light. Could he possibly return some of those feelings? Her head swam in confusion as Gustaf hoisted her up onto the buggy seat in cold silence. Just when she thought she was beginning to understand, his actions contradicted what she'd reasoned in her mind.

Would she ever be able to figure out Gustaf and his intentions?

thirteen

Sunday morning arrived bright and cheerful, yet Raelene was anything but. How could it shine so gaily when clouds of insecurity enveloped her? Raelene's stomach had more knots than the ties and stays of her petticoats and gown. All thumbs in her nervousness, she'd fumbled till her aching arms threatened to fall off before finally getting it right.

Am I overdressed?

She cast a critical eye at the attire she'd selected from her trunk in the loft. It appeared simple enough and certainly wasn't one of her best. But she didn't want to draw any unnecessary attention to herself on her first day in church since the death of her parents. Fastening the lappet cap over her braided and pinned hair, Raelene grabbed her reticule and fan and reached for the door as a firm knock sounded on the other side. A knock she knew all too well.

The stiff man who greeted her was not the Gustaf she'd expected. When she'd agreed to have him escort her to town, she'd anticipated his wounded pride at her interest in Mr. Sanbourne might still plague him, but the foot-shuffling way he avoided her gaze was something else. Dapper enough in clean breeches, a shirt, and waistcoat, he worried the edges of his cocked hat.

"Good. . ." He swallowed several times, causing his Adam's apple to bob up and down over the *casaque* tied at his neck and draped about his shoulders. "Good day, Miss Strattford."

Why was he nervous? She was the prodigal who was likely to be the focus of curious or condemning eyes.

Gustaf gave her a quick appraisal. "I can see you are ready."

Raelene couldn't tell if the slight widening of his eyelids and twitch of his lips was approval or disapproval. Frustrated, she accepted the stiff arm he offered her.

"We go now?"

She almost changed her mind. If not for her friendship with Karianna, she would have. Heaving a long sigh, she nodded. "We go now," she said, although from her demeanor, it might as well have been an execution as a wedding.

The ride to town passed in silence. As Raelene read the black letters on the town sign, memories of past Sunday mornings when she'd looked forward to attending church surfaced. Every week, she had stepped out of the candle shop with her parents and crossed the town green to the church. They'd been a part of the town elite, recognized for their contribution to the community and their military ties to England.

But when they'd become farmers and landowners, their status seemed to shift. Had Father lived, perhaps they could have amassed holdings equal to the Hanssen farm and regained their position. That was now her responsibility. How would those attending services react to her presence? Were they aware that she'd faithfully paid the note on the farm? Or was it more than wagging tongues that made her twist her petticoat until she'd wrinkled it?

Once he'd secured the wagon, Gustaf escorted Raelene to the church and stepped aside so she could enter ahead of him. With more boldness and composure than she felt, she made her way to the pew that her family had occupied since the day they had arrived in town, leaving Gustaf to sit with his family. She didn't want to give the townsfolk more fodder for gossip than her appearance would create. She caught a glimpse of Mr. Sanbourne, but he must have taken note of her stiff demeanor, as he remained where he stood.

Across the center aisle, Kaariana's face beamed at Raelene

with delight. The sight of her friend's pleasure almost made Raelene's battle worthwhile, but it didn't offset the anguish that the empty spaces next to her caused.

It flared full force, drawing her attention from the sermon. All she could feel was the loss. All she could see through the blur of vision was the sparse altar and the shape of the minister.

At long last, it was over with a song Raelene knew but could not sing. Numb, she moved like a sheep with the herd outside to the lawn for the wedding ceremony. She shouldn't have come. What if her grief grew unbearable? She'd ruin the wedding.

When Gustaf appeared on her left, she hardly noticed the mountain of a man for the mountains of responsibility growing in her mind—the debt to be paid, the land to make flourish, and worst of all, the stipulation in the will that she marry.

Seven weeks, and her fate would be decided. . .on her birthday, no less. She'd either be standing where Kaariana now stood or be forced to return to her family in England, her land taken from her and her dreams in tatters.

Kaariana glowed as she faced Jurien. *At least her feelings were considered before her father agreed to the marriage. Not like mine.*

After a brief exchange of vows and a blessing spoken by the reverend, it was done. Karianna and Jurien were man and wife—not because of a contract, but because they wanted to be. They were in love. A shout of "Huzzah!" went up from the small assembly.

"Come, join us as we celebrate this joyous occasion," the reverend announced with his booming voice. "Ample food and wonderful music are provided."

Raelene couldn't move.

The sounds around her melted into dissonance. Faces

blurred and swirled, and she swayed on her feet.

Gustaf immediately steadied her. "Miss Strattford?" Concern laced his voice and filled his eyes.

Raelene placed her gloved palm on his cape. "Please," she managed to whisper, "take me home, Mr. Hanssen. I can bear no more."

She must have looked as desperate as she felt because, thankfully, Raelene didn't have to ask twice.

ও৯

Gustaf helped her down from the wagon. "You will be all right? I can still bring Dr. Schuylar."

The last thing she needed was more people around. Raelene gave his hand a slight squeeze. "As I said in town, Gustaf, I have no need of a doctor. The heat has overwhelmed me, and I need only to rest. Mama had a tea for just such a time. Please, do not worry." *Just leave me alone.* She slipped her fingers from his grasp.

"I remain close if you need me."

Need? What she needed was some peace and quiet. And she wouldn't get it until she eased Gustaf's concern. She was touched, but she didn't want to face the undeniable truths that might come from admitting that.

"Mr. Hanssen, thank you for everything today. Your attentiveness has helped me endure a difficult situation. But now I need some time alone."

Gustaf accepted her wishes, even if he couldn't disguise his reluctance to leave. She watched him lead his horses in the direction of his farm. Alone at last.

But was that what she truly wanted?

She'd thought she did, but faced with isolation, she found the emptiness was unbearable. *This is ridiculous. I'm quite well. I merely need time to gather my senses.* And the best place to do that was with the one friend who had never let her down.

Valdig.

Without a second thought, Raelene made her way to the barn. The familiar smells of hay, oak, and farm animals greeted her. Spending time with Valdig always soothed and comforted her like one of Mama's soft, hand-stitched quilts. He had a way of knowing just what she needed. A gentle whinny showed he was in tune with her even now.

"How are you, boy?" she said as she scratched from his forelock to his nose. He stretched his neck over the gate of his stall and nuzzled her arm.

Laughing with delight, Raelene guided his head away and placed a kiss between his eyes. "Oh, you are quite the rascal. What makes you think I have anything for you?"

Valdig tossed his head and neighed in response as if to say, "You always do."

To prove him right, Raelene withdrew a carrot from the pocket she'd long ago stitched in the folds of the petticoat. Valdig eagerly accepted the treat, his whiskers tickling her palm as his velvet muzzle caressed it. How easy it was to fall back into a routine.

A lone tear slipped from her eye. She reached up to brush it away, and Valdig tipped his nose under her chin. Raelene leaned over the gate and threw her arms around his neck.

"Oh, how I have missed you!"

Valdig settled his head over her shoulder and allowed the embrace, once again knowing just what she needed.

After composing herself, Raelene checked on Jägar and their milking cows. Assured that everything was in order, she latched the barn door and backed away—right into Preston Sanbourne.

Her hand immediately went to her throat as she attempted to catch her breath. A day without an encounter. Was that too much to ask?

"Mr. Sanbourne! You startled me."

"Ah, Miss Strattford. Forgive my intrusion." He bowed low,

but a devilish twinkle in his eyes set Raelene's heart jumping. "I wondered why I didn't see you during the festivities in town, so I decided to find out myself."

His voice had the schooled edge of trying too hard to appear nonchalant.

"Do forgive me, Mr. Sanbourne, but a headache from the heat hastened my departure, and Mr. Hanssen was good enough to bring me home."

"Ah, yes," he replied, his mouth curling without humor. "The *kind* Mr. Hanssen. The overseer present for your every need."

Raelene bristled at the innuendo. "I do not believe I appreciate your insinuations, Mr. Sanbourne. Mr. Hanssen has been nothing but a gentleman in every regard while he has been working here. Which is more than I can say for you at the moment."

Sanbourne remained unaffected by her insult. "Is that any way to speak to someone merely inquiring after your health?" he chided gently.

Be careful, she silently reprimanded. Something about his presence and demeanor suggested he played some sort of game, although what it was or why eluded Raelene. "Perhaps I am not thinking clearly and merely responding out of fatigue."

"Why don't we go for a little walk? I'd like the opportunity to continue our conversation from the other day in town."

"Mr. Sanbourne, I do appreciate the invitation, but as I stated, I suffer from an aching head and am quite overwhelmed from today's events. I would like nothing better than to rest." She started to step around him. "Please excuse me."

He grabbed her wrist, painfully stopping her departure, and pressed her against the stable door. "That isn't how you were supposed to respond."

"Forgive me, Mr. Sanbourne, but—"

"No need to apologize for the attraction I can see in your eyes, no matter what that lovely mouth of yours says."

Raelene's indignation hitched in her throat. She *had* admired the man and his impeccable manner, but—

"There's no cause for fear, dearest," he assured her. "I only intend to make you realize what your eyes already know."

As he leaned toward her, Raelene felt like a cornered animal. Backed up against the barn, she had nowhere to run.

As he lowered his head to hers, Raelene inhaled his hot breath, ready to scream. But before she found her voice, Sanbourne rose off the ground, lifted by unseen hands, and whirled away, stumbling over his own feet and grasping for something to keep from sprawling on the ground.

The roar of Gustaf's voice drew Raelene's attention from her startled assailant to where he stood like a towering god of thunder.

❧

It was all Gustaf could do to keep from tearing off the man's head then and there. The moment he'd seen Sanbourne ride up and walk toward the barn, Gustaf had raced across the field. He'd heard of Sanbourne's less-than-noble plans regarding Raelene while in town that day but hadn't expected the man to make his move so soon.

Momentarily stunned, Preston recovered and hurled himself at Gustaf. "How dare you, you overgrown oaf!"

With a strength born of hard labor, Gustaf deflected Preston's blow and swung at the man's jaw. But he connected with air. Before he realized where the quick-footed scoundrel had gone, a fist shot up, smashing squarely into the ridge of bone over Gustaf's eye. White light flashed, and Gustaf blinked. His vision cleared just as Preston came at him again. Gustaf blocked the jab, his glower backing the man off beyond reach.

"I thought you two were more than just a hired man and

his employer," Sanbourne huffed, his feet moving like a dancer. "Now I know that Miss Strattford isn't quite the lady she professes to—"

Raging like a bull, Gustaf charged and swung, but once again his adversary dodged him. "Stand still, you coward," he demanded. "This is a fight, not a jig."

"And this is boxing, you muscle-bound imbecile."

Blood pounding in his temples, Gustaf plowed into the man again and, once again, Sanbourne danced away, but not before delivering a stabbing kidney punch. "You'll not lay a hand—"

Ignoring what felt like a steel blade twisting in his back, Gustaf spun on the man with a powerful hook, proving him wrong. The impact practically lifted Sanbourne off the ground, and he descended in a crumpled heap. Walking over to the fallen man, his chest heaving, Gustaf seethed. "You stay off this farm. I give fair warning."

"I—I think you've broken my jaw," Sanbourne slurred as he pulled himself up on the nearby post.

"It could have been your neck," Gustaf replied without sympathy. "And it will be your neck if you hint that Miss Strattford is anything less than a lady. Am I clear?" he called after Sanbourne, who staggered toward his horse without looking back.

"Quite," he managed to respond.

Gustaf watched the unwelcome visitor until he was mounted and headed away from the homestead, holding back the murderous rage that still rampaged through his veins. Had Sanbourne not given up when he did—

Gustaf doubled over at the waist and pressed his fists into his sides, taking in huge gulps of air to calm himself. His body trembled, and the pain his fury had overridden made itself known. Yet even as his brain acknowledged it, soft cries from a few feet away beat it back into submission again. Raelene!

He rushed to where Raelene huddled against the stable wall, her body shaking with strangled sobs. Kneeling in the dirt beside her, he laid a hand on her arm.

"*Min raring*, Raelene."

She answered his "*My dear*" with what sounded like a combination between a hiccup and a gasp, giving him cause for concern that maybe he'd overstepped his bounds.

"*Var god*—" He checked himself, switching to English for fear it might come too naturally in his native language to reveal more of his feelings than he dared.

"Please. He is gone."

Lifting her head, Raelene sniffled but kept her eyes downcast.

"You are safe."

He retrieved a handkerchief and pressed it into her hands. This was becoming a habit, one that wasn't altogether unpleasant.

"It was my f—fault," she murmured brokenly. "I—I must have been too friendly in town—"

"Nonsense," Gustaf objected. "He is no gentleman. He is a wolf in sheep's clothing. Never your fault," he vowed softly, stroking away a golden strand of hair from her face. "I do not want to hear that."

After wiping her cheeks and eyes, Raelene raised her gaze to his. Her eyes widened. "You're bleeding!"

Surprised, he reached up to touch the tender spot near his eye.

"No! Don't touch it. It could become infected."

As though she drew strength from his injuries, Raelene hurried to her feet and grabbed his arm, all but dragging him over to a worktable. She rummaged through an odd assortment of supplies and selected the ones she wanted.

Gustaf watched in disbelief. She was going to tend to his wounds with the same bandages and ointments she used on

Jägar and Valdig. And he was going to let her.

Focused on tending to him, she didn't even pause to meet his gaze before beginning her ministrations. With ointment on a cloth, she raised it to his temple.

"You do not have to do this," he mumbled halfheartedly. "I will take care of it."

"No!" she said a little too fast. "P–please. I m–must do this. I owe you this much."

The pleading in her eyes and tremble in her voice made him consent. But it was more than that. Her eyes were saying "Stay away," while her touch was saying "Thank you" and "Don't go." A compelling contrast that fascinated him.

Gustaf remained still as she cleaned the cut at his temple. With Raelene at such close proximity, an acute awareness overcame him. The faint scent of lavender mixed with the scent of horseflesh and ointment caused an odd but heady sensation, enough to make him think things he had no right—

"I wanted. . ."

Raelene's soft words jerked him away from his unsettling thoughts, but she hesitated. After a moment, she spoke again.

"I must thank you for today." Raelene focused on her task and avoided his eyes. "If you had not arrived when you did, I—" Her words caught in her throat. "I cannot bear to think what Mr. Sanbourne would have done."

A shudder overtook her, leaving her trembling in its wake. Every fiber in him wanted to pull Raelene into his arms and hold her, stilling her fear. He clenched his fists and forced his arms to remain at his side as he watched a range of emotions cross her face. Gratefulness, panic, trepidation, agitation, and finally, control. When she moved to clean the cut at the corner of his mouth, he nearly lost his own. Surely his teeth would crack if he clenched his jaw any tighter.

What he wouldn't give to know what Raelene was thinking.

If she was half as aware of him as she was of her, she must have better control than he.

Her fingers grazed his lips, causing him to inhale a sharp breath.

She froze.

Her touch both unnerved him and awakened his senses. He placed his left hand over hers. It shook as he raised it to his mouth, but she did not resist. At its contact, liquid fire surged through his veins.

"Raelene." The guttural quality of his voice surprised him. Her widened eyes suggested that she, too, was shocked, making him want to take it back. But when those blue pools met his, her shock softened and a soulful light shone from their depths. With his other hand, he cupped her cheek. Raelene inhaled a tremulous breath, her lips parting. A lump the size of his fist formed in Gustaf's throat.

Slowly, he lowered her hand from his mouth and leaned forward. Her eyelids fluttered closed and her hand tensed, but she didn't try to remove it from his. All he could think about was what it would be like to taste her lips. Just before Gustaf's mouth found hers, Duncan Strattford's words came to him. *"Promise you'll take care of her. Promise me you won't let her get hurt."*

Someone may as well have dumped a bucket of cold water over his head. With a jerk, Gustaf moved away and dropped her hand.

Raelene stared, confusion and hurt clouding her eyes.

"I—I cannot," he stammered. "I make promise. And I will not break it."

Her crestfallen face was nearly his undoing. He almost closed the gap between them and picked up where he'd left off. But it wouldn't be right. He'd pay the consequences of his actions, and so would she.

With a groan borne of frustration, Gustaf retreated,

barreling out of the barn. The responsibility that her father had placed on his shoulders was almost unbearable. And from the wounded look she'd given him, it was impossible. No matter what he did, he seemed destined to hurt the one person he'd not hurt for the world. Never mind that she'd seemed to welcome his attention, making his blood boil in the process. What he needed was a cold dip in the creek. Although it wouldn't clear his mind of the hurt on Raelene's face. His was an impossible situation.

fourteen

In mute shock, Raelene watched Gustaf leave. One minute, she was tending his wounds, and the next, they were both locked in a place where time didn't matter. Then, as if a lightning bolt had touched ground nearby, he'd started, snatching the magic from her, as well.

He could've at least said good-bye. . .something. Yet her irritation at Gustaf paled in comparison to what had almost happened, what she had almost let happen. Shame filled her, and she pressed her hands to her warm cheeks.

"You are safe."

Those were the same words he'd uttered when he'd brought her parents home after their accident. The compassion in his blue eyes filled her with an odd mixture of assurance and comfort. The same had happened just now. But nothing about her feelings for him was safe or comfortable.

She crumpled in a heap of petticoats on the loose clumps of hay at her feet and sobbed. How could she have let things reach this point? The attraction. The awareness. The desire. If he hadn't walked away, she wouldn't have been able to stop him.

Thankfully, Gustaf *had* walked away. Two advances in one day were more than enough, even if one wasn't entirely unwanted.

Composing herself, Raelene gently wiped the tears from her cheeks with the soft linen of Gustaf's handkerchief. It filled her nose with his outdoorsy scent. Ignoring the resulting ache within, Raelene filled her lungs to calm her erratic breathing.

Jägar's nicker from the stall closest to her drew her attention away from her distress. The gentle way Jägar looked at her made it feel like Papa was there, empathizing with her. She wanted to believe it was so with all her heart, for it comforted her like nothing else could.

But in her confusion about men and love, she supposed she needed Mama's presence more. And if she listened to her senses rather than her longing heart, she was exactly where she'd been the moment they left—alone.

Raelene stood and brushed the straw from her skirts. As she made her way to the cottage, she glanced at the fields, wondering where Gustaf had gone. With not even a shadow in the distance, she stepped inside.

It was just as well. They needed time apart to gather their wits and get back on the right path. The path they'd both chosen from the start.

As her eyes adjusted to the dark interior of her home, Raelene paused. It was silly, she knew, but her longing to connect with her mother overrode reason. Perhaps if she did work that she'd often done with Mama. . .

Raelene frowned, lost in thought. Other than candle making, Mama had only one other interest that drew her into the room with Raelene.

Embroidery.

Raelene went to the cedar chest in Mama's room and retrieved the quilt squares from the heavy-scented interior. Settling into the rocking chair by the hearth, she draped Mama's half-finished creation across her lap, grabbed supplies from the basket at her feet, and set to work.

The familiar in-and-out motion as she pushed and pulled the needle and thread brought comfort in the routine. Mama always said that needlework soothed the mind and rested the soul. *"Try to keep a straight line,"* Mama would always say. *"And pull tight. You do not want your work unraveling."*

Raelene's smile faded as she spied the dented tin cup Gustaf always used. Once again, thoughts of Gustaf and how she'd responded to him plagued her. If only she could talk to memories, confide in Mama. Grief fell unchecked, soaking into the dry fabric in her lap.

"Oh, Mama! Why did you and Papa leave me here alone? I've made a dreadful mess of things, and I need your counsel."

Unable to run from what had happened in the barn, Raelene steeled herself. She'd go over it step by step until she understood why she'd felt like kissing away Gustaf's pain and falling into his strong arms.

She had been agitated by Preston's attempts to compromise her. Then the intimacy of tending to Gustaf's wounds had led to agitation of a different sort. How could she not have seen to him? He'd come to her rescue and defended her honor. It was the least she could do.

It couldn't be attraction because Gustaf wasn't her idea of a suitable husband. Gustaf was a farmer. He was her overseer. His involvement in her life was for the sole purpose of helping her establish her farm, so she could turn a good profit and settle the note to her land. And of course to help her find a husband. Once that happened, he could go back to his farm or leave to find land of his own, and she'd never have to see him again.

It was what they both wanted, she told herself, ignoring the painful squeeze around her heart. It was the only solution possible. Not that Gustaf wasn't a good man. When he didn't allow his anger to reign, he had a peace that she hadn't known in a long time.

No matter how many times she allowed her arrogance to control her words, he almost always took the blame. But not without also delivering chastisement in the form of advice.

"Getting angry at me and others who help you, Raelene, will make you more unhappy. If you continue in your haughty ways, you will have no one left."

"At least he admits I'm not the only one at fault." Raelene pushed the needle through the quilt square and pulled tight from the other side. Gustaf had wisdom and character, making him far from the buffoon that Sanbourne had accused him of being. The things the man had said to Gustaf were so degrading.

Raelene's eyes widened. That's what it was. It was *empathy*, not attraction.

She'd been appalled by Sanbourne's pretentiousness and condescension, and hurt for Gustaf. Despite the occasional stilted English and his unrefined social skills, Gustaf managed quite well with the life he lived.

People simply weren't as formal here in the colonies. Raelene remembered when Mama and Papa first introduced her to their neighbors in town. Although New Castle was similar to home with its cobbled streets, shops, and town square, the populace was different. Raelene thought initially that the community was lacking in something.

Pretentiousness.

Oh, there were some who insisted upon making everyone aware of their lofty position in town, but for the most part, everyone here understood that life wasn't easy in the colonies. Things they might have taken for granted back home weren't available. Everyone looked out for everyone else. There was no room for arrogance if one wanted real friends like Gustaf had in abundance. Like she was sorely bereft of.

"Gustaf was so right then," Raelene groaned aloud. "My manners were deplorable where he and his family were concerned." But she'd made an attempt to improve.

And she had. Maybe that was why he'd looked at her so keenly in that magical moment in the barn. He'd seen the change in her and was moved by it. She no longer believed that he only helped her for her land. Raelene understood that his sense of honor kept him working for her.

He truly had nothing to gain by staying—and so much to gain had he not. He could be following his dream, maybe have found his own farm by now. Yet he stayed, determined to make her farm flourish and to help her keep it by finding her a suitable husband. But with less than two months until her birthday, was that a possibility? Raelene clutched the quilt blocks to her chest, closing her eyes as though she might see the future.

If only she knew.

ىە

The horses neighed in greeting as Gustaf entered the barn a few hours later. Free of his leather jerkin, the ends of his shirt hung loose over his breeches, and he hadn't bothered to fasten the snaps of his stockings. That dip in the creek had done a world of good in cooling him off. But it didn't remove the memory of Raelene's face inches from his own or the flash of emotion he'd seen just before her eyelids drifted shut.

She'd wanted his kiss as much as he'd wanted to give it. That was why he had to stay away. If he allowed his feelings to take control, any chance she had of making a good match would be ruined. Worse, he'd break his promise to her father, something he could never do.

Jerking free two fistfuls of fresh hay, he strode toward the four horses and offered them each a treat. Gustaf scratched their forelocks as they chewed.

"Why can't I stay away and do my work?"

That never got him into any trouble, and he could do that without worrying about whether his actions would jeopardize their agreement.

"It is good you two cause me no problems." Gustaf patted the jowls of Jägar and Valdig. He released a disdainful chuckle. "Now I talk to horses. I must be mad." After making his way up to the hayloft, he stared out the opening at the clear sky as night descended. The twinkling lights seemed to be talking to each other. If only they'd offer him advice on his predicament. But only One could do that.

"God above," he said to the sky. "You have a purpose for me here. I stay because I believe this. But I made a big mistake. I don't want that mistake to hurt Raelene. She needs You, not me. Please show her that."

"Trust Me."

The words seemed to fill the barn. At first, he wondered if one of the animals had been given a voice like the donkey in the Bible. But then he recognized God's voice.

"You have remained faithful and will be rewarded."

The promise spoke to his heart and gave him a relief he hadn't felt in weeks. He should have spoken with God more often. Maybe that incident in the barn wouldn't have happened if he had. It was over now, and he could get back to what he did best. Farming.

At least in that, he had confidence.

※

Rising early the next morning, Gustaf concealed his blanket and the old shirt he used as a pillow. He didn't need Raelene venturing into the hayloft and finding his bed. Although he was certain Preston wouldn't pose a threat any longer, he didn't feel right leaving Raelene alone on the farm.

With the bedclothes away, he set about his morning chores. Selecting a couple of apples, Gustaf used the fruit and a few pieces of dried jerky to break the fast. He couldn't bring himself to approach the cottage, regardless of the tantalizing smells that wafted toward him. His stomach groaned in response, but he ignored it and dove into his work with a vengeance.

By midmorning, he'd given up trying to turn his thoughts away from Raelene. She'd opened the back door to the cottage to dispose of the remnants of whatever meal she'd cooked. From a distance, Gustaf watched as she worked in her garden and disappeared inside again a couple of hours later. No matter what he did, her face wasn't far from his mind.

Striking the anvil with the mallet, he pounded with such force that he didn't hear anything else until he noticed a horse and rider come to a stop beside the cottage. Gustaf paused and shifted his gaze between the unfamiliar man, who dismounted with the ease of a skilled rider, and the cottage, its back door firmly shut.

Obviously, Raelene either hadn't heard the horse or was ignoring it and leaving it to him to greet the visitor. The least he could do was introduce himself and offer the man a drink.

Gustaf pulled his hair back and retied the string. He might be simply a farmer, but he was representing Raelene's farm and should look presentable. Wiping his hands on his breeches, he approached the man with hand extended.

"I am Gustaf Hanssen. I work as the overseer. You have come to see Miss Strattford?"

Although an inch or two shy of Gustaf's height, the man carried himself well and possessed an air of confidence. Yet something in his demeanor bespoke a humility that others who had come to visit lacked. That was one point in his favor. He seemed to be about Gustaf's age.

"From what I hear in town, you are the one I need to see first." The man accepted Gustaf's handshake. "Cedric Milton." He cast an eye around the farm and looked out over the fields. "You have done a fine job of working this farm. When I learned of Miss Strattford's most unfortunate loss, I had wondered how she would manage. This is quite impressive."

Gustaf liked this man. Genteel, but genuine, he treated Gustaf as an equal. So why was he here?

"I must say I did not expect to find myself in this position, but I cannot speak falsely and say it does not have its benefits. It seems to be a gift from God that I returned home when I did."

What was this man saying? Had Gustaf missed something that would explain the odd words Cedric spoke? Gustaf's face must have shown his confusion, because Cedric immediately became contrite.

He swept his cocked hat from his head and slapped it

against his chest. "Oh, do forgive me. We have only just met, so how could you possibly know anything of my past acquaintance with Miss Strattford?"

Past acquaintance? "You and Miss Strattford. You met her before?"

"Yes, but our families only had a brief time together before I had to depart. Her family had recently arrived in New Castle and her father had purchased the candle shop." Cedric's horse whinnied softly, interrupting their conversation. "I do not wish to impose, but would you have some fresh water for my horse?"

Gustaf mentally chastised himself. Where were his manners? He'd become so distracted by the respect Cedric gave him, offering to water the horse had slipped his mind. "Yes. We have a large barn with extra room for your horse. He will have fresh hay and water to drink."

Cedric followed his lead. So the man had already met Raelene, albeit a few years ago. And he'd been away for some time. How much did he know about the stipulations surrounding Raelene's inheritance? His fine horse and clothing suggested he wasn't here for her money, but what other reason did her previous suitors have?

After leading his horse into the barn, Cedric turned to face Gustaf. "I suppose I should start at the beginning."

Gustaf nodded.

Cedric held the reins of his steed loosely, allowing it to drink its fill from the trough. "As I said, I met Miss Strattford and her family when they first arrived. I was working as an apprentice for the owner of the dry goods shop while also assisting my father with our farm. I had only six months left before my apprenticeship was complete." He ran his hand along the dark, shiny neck of his animal. "Once I finished, I planned to purchase land and start my own farm. Then Mother became quite ill. It didn't take long before we realized she wouldn't be long on this earth."

"I am sorry."

Cedric slanted an appreciative glance his way. "Thank you. It wasn't an easy time, but I am quite thankful the good Lord spared her pain and took her quickly."

The good Lord. Pleasure filled Gustaf at Cedric giving credit to God for his mother's release from pain. One more point in his favor.

"After her passing, Father and I sailed home to England to settle affairs there. Unfortunately, some complications and family disputes forced us to remain there for more than a year. Father wasn't able to make the journey back here, so I returned alone." Melancholy overtook his expression. "Now I must decide whether to sell or develop the family farm. Our indentured servants and overseer tended to the farm while we were away, but I now have full charge and must make a decision." He took a deep, bracing breath. "Which brings me here."

Now it was starting to make sense to Gustaf. "You want to speak with Miss Strattford. If she agrees, you will sell your farm and work this one instead?"

"That is a possibility." His reply came out in a whoosh of relief.

"This can be done with my pleasure. I will make the introductions."

Gustaf straightened as a shadow crossed the doorway to the barn.

"Make introductions to whom?"

Clothed in simple cotton with her hair braided beneath her lappet cap, Raelene was a breath of fresh air in the barn. Her familiar lavender scent drifted along the breeze from outside, reminding Gustaf of how close he'd come to kissing her the day before, of how much he wanted Raelene for himself. Could he go through with this? A minute ago, he had believed Cedric was an answer to prayer. With Raelene standing a few feet away, he wasn't so sure.

Thankfully, the choice wasn't up to him.

Raelene held out his handkerchief. "I came to return this to you."

When he took the freshly washed and folded fabric from her, his gaze locked with hers. Did she remember, or was what he'd hoped was mutual attraction simply gratitude? When Cedric quietly cleared his throat, Gustaf realized how long he'd stood there like a tongue-tied fool.

"Miss Strattford, this is Cedric Milton. He has come to meet you again."

Raelene's smooth brow rose in surprise, but a small measure of recognition also appeared on her face. "Again?" she asked, eyeing the man with open curiosity.

"Yes, Miss Strattford, again." Cedric wiped his hands with a clean handkerchief and tucked it away before extending a hand to her.

"We met when your family first arrived in New Castle. I was just telling Mr. Hanssen why I've been away for so long. But I am home now and would like very much to call upon you. If you agree, I shall share with you that story, as well, and perhaps hear of your three years since first arriving in this fine colony." Cedric backed away so that he addressed both Raelene and Gustaf before continuing. "I apologize for not coming to the cottage first, but I believed speaking with Mr. Hanssen beforehand was the proper thing to do."

He was polished and mannerly. Gustaf had to give him that. And he'd obviously impressed Raelene. From the way her face lit up, Cedric was just the type of gentleman that Raelene had spoken of when she'd told Gustaf of her childhood dreams. Now that such a man was standing here in the flesh, Gustaf should be happy for her, but he was not.

"Yes," she said. "You may call again at your convenience. I would be delighted to learn more."

Of course she would be delighted. Being everything that Gustaf wasn't made Cedric all the more attractive.

"Would my arrival upon the morrow be too soon?"

Yes! Gustaf wanted to exclaim. But he held his tongue.

"Tomorrow would be fine. I shall expect you around midday." Her face flushed pink as a rose, Raelene curtsied, gave their visitor a dazzling smile, and retreated with a step that seemed lighter than Gustaf could recall. If this brief meeting was any indication, he and Raelene would be seeing a lot more of Mr. Milton.

As Cedric mounted to leave, it was all Gustaf could do to sound as if he, too, looked forward to their visitor's return. If Cedric won Raelene's heart, Gustaf would at least be free to pursue his own dreams. So why did it feel as though he were looking forward to a prison sentence rather than freedom?

fifteen

Raelene accepted Cedric's assistance as she stepped down from his buggy. He held on to her hand a little longer than necessary, but she didn't mind. This had been their fourth outing together in a little over a week. With him at her side, she'd managed to attend Sunday services again. She'd finally found someone who didn't bore or offend her with his self-serving demeanor.

"Thank you for a most enjoyable outdoor excursion, Mr. Milton. Walking along the banks of the Christina used to be a favorite pastime of mine. Lately, there hasn't been time."

Cedric raised her hand to his lips and brushed a feathery light kiss across her knuckles. "The pleasure was all mine, I assure you." He straightened and met her gaze. "Your pleasant company only added to the delight of this fine day." Reaching into the buggy, he retrieved the basket he'd stowed. "And the meal you provided was fit for a king."

Raelene raised a gloved hand to her mouth, unable to hold back a girlish giggle at his flattery.

"Would you care for tea? You do have a rather long journey back to your farm."

He tucked the basket into the crook of his arm. "Thank you. I do believe I will accept your invitation."

"You can set the basket on the bench," Raelene instructed before stepping inside the cottage. "Tea will be ready in a few moments."

After she placed the teakettle over the fire, Raelene sat on the footstool and stoked the banked embers. Cedric entered and approached the bookshelf along the opposite wall, his hands clasped behind his back. He wasn't what she'd consider handsome, but he did have attractive qualities. She leaned back to observe his profile. Strong, but with a less rigid pose that paralleled his gentle nature. Not like the hard set of Gustaf's angular jaw.

Raelene stiffened. Where had that thought come from? Just when she thought she could separate her business affairs from her personal life, the line between them blurred with Gustaf sitting astride it. Oh, that infuriating man!

The water in the teakettle rattled the lid and forced Raelene's attention back to the task at hand. Anything to keep her mind off Gustaf. She poured tea for Cedric and herself, then preceded him outside to the bench and searched for words to hide her discomfort.

"I wanted to tell you how much I appreciate your invitations and company. They have been a welcome respite from the daily chores and routine."

His lips curved up. "I do hope your acceptance of my visits has been out of more than mere gratitude."

Raelene reached for her fan and snapped it open, partially obscuring her face. "For truth, sir, what other reason could there be?"

"Why, my dashing nature, of course," he supplied with a twinkle in his eyes.

Oh, he was so much like her cousins with his charming wit. Spending time with him reminded her of the fun they used to have and of the carefree way she felt with Kaariana. Cedric had mentioned spending the past year in England. How was it that some maiden there hadn't captured his attention? If only she felt more than friendship for him.

Cedric set down his cup and clasped her free hand in his, an intent look replacing the jovial one. "I do hope you realize my intentions are honorable."

Raelene grew so stiff that she could only nod.

He cast a quick glance around, as though looking for Gustaf's giant shadow, which was always about, then returned his earnest gaze to her. "And as the sun has halfway completed its descent, I must hasten in posing this next question."

Her heartbeat thudded in her chest. What was he going to ask? They'd been reacquainted for less than two weeks. Surely he wouldn't—

"Would you do me the honor of accompanying me to town next week to attend a special service? A traveling preacher whose words have sparked a fire among colonists from here to Boston will speak. If you are in agreement, I would like to escort you."

Preacher? Oh, bother! That meant another sermon and more talk of God. Yet despite her previous aversion to spiritual matters, part of her warmed to the idea. Perhaps Gustaf's constant lectures were getting through, after all.

"I would like to give the matter some thought. I will provide an answer when you arrive to escort me to Sunday services."

Cedric finished the last of his tea. "I shall eagerly await your reply." He stood and retrieved his hat. "Now I shall bid you good evening and take my leave."

She walked with him to his buggy and waited as he climbed onto the seat and took the reins.

"I count the days until Sunday arrives." After touching two fingers to the edge of his hat, he drove off.

Such gentlemanly conduct and strict adherence to social graces. Yet for all his appeal, Cedric didn't stir her heart. Not like—

The loud clatter of wood pieces tumbling against each other interrupted Raelene's musings. She peered around the corner of the cottage to find Gustaf loading his arms with another stack of wood as he transferred it from the wheelbarrow to the pile. Never far from her in thought or proximity, Gustaf once again had managed to invade and confuse her mind.

However, Gustaf had kept his distance since Cedric had entered her life. Even on the days when she was alone on the farm, he no longer joined her for the noon meal or suggested they continue with their reading. Conversation remained at a minimum, though he always made sure she knew he was close by should she need him.

And while she hadn't needed him, she had missed his company.

Grabbing the water pail, she headed toward him. As she approached, Gustaf paused with several logs stacked against his chest. Raelene couldn't help but admire the way the fabric of his shirt stretched across his broad shoulders and taut muscles. His masculine scent mixed with the sweat of hard labor wafted her way, stirring her in a way that Cedric's tonic and soap never did. But Mr. Milton suited her taste far more, didn't he?

"Your outing today. You enjoyed it?"

Raelene blinked several times and focused on Gustaf's question. "Yes, very much so. Mr. Milton and I walked along the river. He entertained me with stories of his time in England and about his family."

Gustaf grabbed a few more logs, then tossed them on the pile like they were twigs. He didn't appear winded from the exertion. "You are happy, then?"

He'd done it again. Caught her with her mind wandering. And with a question like the one he'd just asked, she needed to stay alert. Her future might depend on the answer. She clasped her hands in front of the pail and hugged it to her.

"Yes," she replied with caution.

His expression remained impassive, but he clenched his jaw, and a vein protruded at the side of his neck. For a moment, he held her gaze; then he returned to his work, seemingly displeased.

But unlike his opinion of the other men who'd expressed interest in her, he condoned Cedric's courtship. *Why doesn't he just speak his mind?* she wondered in frustration. Then again, why didn't she?

"I enjoy visiting with Mr. Milton. It is a refreshing change from the daily routine around the farm." That was honest enough.

What appeared to be a flash of hurt crossed Gustaf's face, but it disappeared so quickly that Raelene wasn't sure she had seen it at all. Surely he didn't think she meant that she enjoyed her day with Cedric more than the noon meals she and Gustaf had often shared. Those times formed a friendship that would forever be treasured. Feeling tongue-tied about her relationship with Gustaf, Raelene skipped to her present quandary.

"I wonder if I might ask your opinion."

Gustaf rested one arm on the growing pile of chopped logs, affording her his full attention.

"Mr. Milton invited me to accompany him to town next week. A visiting preacher is arriving, and he wishes to escort me to the services."

Surprise registered on Gustaf's face. He regarded her for several moments. Raelene shifted from one foot to the other. If he didn't say something soon, she would start rambling.

"You wish to hear this preacher?"

His voice and expression contained a blend of hope and interest. At least he should be pleased that his talk of God the past few months might come to some fruition.

Raelene stared into the pail she held, its emptiness mirroring the realities of her own life. Avoiding Gustaf's intent gaze, she answered, "I realize it might come as a surprise, but I have heard of these meetings and read about them in the *Gazette*. Many are getting excited about these men who come speaking of revival and lighting fires that cannot be quenched. Mr. Milton seemed quite interested. If one of them is coming to New Castle, I do not want to miss the opportunity to hear him for myself."

"It is good to hear and make your own opinion and not build it on what other people say."

Raelene raised her head. "Then you think I should go?"

Gustaf stepped to the side of the woodpile. "You should go for you, not anyone else. You need an open mind. If your heart tells you to go, then go. Do not go to make someone else happy."

He was right. If she went to please Cedric or Gustaf, she'd be going for the wrong reasons.

"Thank you, Gustaf," she said softly. "You are a treasured friend. But will you also be in attendance?"

"Yes. I go with my family." His stilted reply gave her pause. He looked as though he were going to say more.

When he remained silent, Raelene slackened her hold on the bucket and allowed it to swing at her side. "I shall see you there."

"I. . ." He hesitated, as though weighing his words. "I pray you hear what you need."

Dear Gustaf and his constant reference to a fix-it-all God! He hadn't fixed her dilemmas. No one was going to explain her confusion about Gustaf and Cedric or move her heart to trust again. But Gustaf was sincere, and his prayers demonstrated his concern for her. She should be grateful, not prickling for an argument.

She fought down her annoyance, uncertain if its cause was Gustaf or God. "Thank you, Gustaf. Your prayers will be welcome."

Raelene stepped around the wheelbarrow and felt Gustaf's dumbstruck gaze follow her. Her heart smiled with more than satisfaction. She'd vowed to change her ways and to start with Gustaf. This moment—while small in the scheme of things—was a triumph, one that made Raelene like herself more than she had in a very long time.

☙

A large gathering had formed in the town hall the following Tuesday to welcome the preacher. The assembly decided to hold the meeting there because the church wouldn't be large enough. After a perusal of her neighbors and of others she didn't recognize, Raelene returned her attention to the man at the front.

"'And a man shall be as an hiding place from the wind, and a covert from the tempest; as rivers of water in a dry place, as the shadow of a great rock in a weary land.'"

Jonathan Edwards's words stirred Raelene. A spark that had long lain dormant flickered.

"The soul of every man necessarily craves happiness. Men in their fallen state are in very great want of this happiness." He had the gift of eloquence, despite his booming voice that rattled through Raelene's ears.

"You are happy, then?"

Gustaf's question came back to her unbidden. Was she? Craving happiness wasn't foreign to her, but had she found it?

"They were once in the enjoyment of it, but mankind has sunk to a very low estate." Edwards paced back and forth, his steps punctuating his words. No wonder men like him had been stirring the souls of colonists in every major town and settlement. Raelene's soul responded to his accusation and admitted the truth in it.

"We are naturally like the prodigal, for we once were rich, but we departed from our Father's house, and have squandered away our wealth, and have become poor, hungry, famishing wretches."

Raelene heard evidence of the stricter confines of his Puritan heritage in his hard-hitting truths rather than the Anglican roots prevalent in the region. But his words contained a basic truth that crossed all beliefs. If the fires of conviction spread to the southern colonies as well, every scalawag from Savannah to Boston would confess his dirty deeds and repent. And Raelene wouldn't be far behind them.

"There is quiet rest and sweet refreshment in Christ for God's people who are weary."

The message chipped away at the walls around Raelene's heart. Rest. Refreshment. Weariness. She knew that last one well. The others she craved like a storm-tossed seaman seeking harbor. Lately, she'd felt battered and tossed, waiting for a calm that never seemed to come.

" 'O God, thou art my God; early will I seek thee: my soul thirsteth for thee, my flesh longeth for thee in a dry and thirsty land, where no water is.'"

Reverend Edwards quoted from the Sixty-third Psalm. Despite Raelene's neglect of what used to be daily reading of the Bible, her heart and mind remembered. Papa used to quote that verse often when she asked him why he went outside to pray before the sun rose every morning.

Suddenly, the reverend appeared to be looking straight at her. Or through her.

"You have a choice to make. You can choose to lean on God for all the strength you need to get you through the travails of life, or you can shrivel and die like a branch cut from a tree. With the connection to the source severed, there is no chance for real life to exist."

It was as though her heart were exposed, laid out for all to see. It beat loudly, crying out her deepest secrets to this man of God. In that moment, no one else mattered. Then, just as quickly, he resumed his sermon.

But the silent message had been clear. It was as though God had commanded him to speak directly to her with words meant for her alone.

"And ye shall seek me, and find me, when ye shall search for me with all your heart."

The remainder of his message contained many more points, each one cutting deep, but that one stood out in her mind. Almost like a voice speaking the words from the book of Jeremiah aloud, the promise offered hope to Raelene's weary soul.

Cedric shifted in his seat on the hard, wooden bench and drew her attention. Like others gathered, his face reflected the enjoyment of the sermon, but his eyes lacked the strong awareness she felt straight to her core.

When Cedric caught her staring through a blur of emotion, he reached across her lap and took one of her hands in his, patting it with familiarity and reassurance. Although he intended to comfort, it paled in comparison to the promise in Jonathan Edwards's words. Or those from her conversations with Gustaf.

Dear Gustaf. Of its own accord, her gaze sought him out and found him watching her intently from his standing position along the far wall. A well of joy sprang from within, silently declaring her revelation across the distance and kindling a spark of hope in Gustaf's eyes—until he looked away like a child caught with his hand in the bread cupboard.

In the periphery of her gaze, Raelene saw Cedric's raised brow and groaned inwardly. It was bad enough her mind had drifted to Gustaf in the middle of the meeting. For Cedric to discover the source of her distraction was far worse.

But distracted she was. Even though she pretended to cling to every syllable Edwards spoke, Gustaf's words echoed in her mind. *"I pray you hear what you need."*

God had answered his prayer, Raelene realized. What was she going to do about it?

☙

On the ride home, Raelene couldn't dislodge the words from the sermon that insisted on replaying in her mind like an echo bouncing off the walls of an empty house. Only the house that held her heart wasn't empty. It was full of hope and the first signs of peace since before her parents had died. She'd all but shut off access to that area of her heart—until this evening.

"Christ gives Himself to His people to be all things to them that they need and all things that make for their happiness."

All things. Everything she needed. At one time in her life, He had been. Could He be again?

As Cedric brought the team and wagon to a stop in front

of her cottage, panic seized her. Should she share her inner struggle with him? How would he react to knowing her faith had been fragile at best? They'd spent a lot of time together over the past weeks, but Raelene wasn't sure she could trust him with matters of the soul.

Cedric saved her the trouble. Rather than climbing down from the seat, he stood to help her descend. When her feet touched ground, he held on to her gloved hand.

"I must apologize for my hasty departure, Miss Strattford, but there is another matter to which I must attend this evening. I fear some of my financial investments will be lost, otherwise."

Raelene forced a cheery smile she didn't feel. "There is no need for apologies, Mr. Milton." She covered her mouth to hide a yawn. "Mr. Edwards's sermon, while long and taxing, has given me much to ponder. Spending the remainder of the evening alone to consider his message is a welcome prospect."

Relief relaxed the worried lines across his brow and allowed the stiffness in his shoulders to ease. "Your understanding is greatly appreciated. Might I be permitted to call again tomorrow?"

"Around noon?"

"Yes."

"I shall see you for the midday meal. Good evening, Mr. Milton."

After Cedric left, the eerie quiet that ensued brought back the distressing key points from the sermon full force. She kept seeing herself as a dried and brittle tree branch on the ground rather than a flourishing tree full of life. Hoping to keep the anguish at bay, Raelene tended to chores before heading inside as the sun disappeared behind the trees and the air took on a chill. As she sat alone with Mama's quilt blocks, in the chair in front of the fireplace, Reverend Edwards's voice filled her mind once again.

"Christ is not only a remedy for your weariness and trouble, but

He will give you an abundance of the contrary: joy and delight."

How long had it been since she had laughed? When was the last time she had the prospect of lasting joy and delight?

Sure, she'd smiled and shared in Gustaf's happiness when the first signs of a successful crop appeared, and again when the hailstorm had spared those same crops. She'd also enjoyed reading from her books at midday and discovering the world of Robinson Crusoe with Gustaf.

All with Gustaf. Raelene smiled. Yet even that joy was overshadowed by fear of what tomorrow might bring.

As for Cedric. . .granted, he was attentive and sincere, a perfect gentleman, and clearly committed to her, as well as to God. He made her laugh with his delightful accounts of life back in London and his wit. But his levity was shallow, not as soul moving as that promised by God's Word.

Gustaf, despite his infuriating stubbornness, had that joy in faith. He lived his faith every day. Even when he failed, he clung to it with the certainty of forgiveness from his loving heavenly Father. And Gustaf had passed that love on to her by giving aid and comfort in her time of need, even when she'd not been very appreciative. He had nothing to gain from all his hard work, yet he offered it freely, just as God offered His love and forgiveness.

Finally, it all made sense. Even though she'd been furious at God, the peace and joy she so longed for was hers for the asking. All she had to do was surrender to Him.

A log fell in the fireplace, and the ensuing sparks lit up the main room. It was as if a veil had been lifted. She understood what Gustaf had been telling her, what her father had told her as he lay dying. God was with her. He'd never left. She was the one who needed to embrace Him again.

Six months ago, Raelene's uncompromising trust in God had faltered. Oh, she still believed that Jesus was God's Son and that He'd died on the cross for her sins—that hadn't changed. But the issue of trust had changed. No longer had she cast all her cares upon the Lord. At her father's deathbed, the scales had been tipped in the other direction. She had reclaimed responsibility for her own well-being. God had fallen short of her expectations, so she no longer trusted in His provision.

"Lord, thou hast been our dwelling place in all generations." The words from the Ninetieth Psalm came to mind and offered Raelene the comfort she'd been seeking. *All* generations. He'd always been there, and He always would be. She could trust Him. Excitement bubbled inside of her, begging for release. She wanted to tell someone, to share her joy. The stillness inside the cottage reminded her. She was alone.

"You are never alone."

Peace filled her at the promise. God felt as real as the needle and thread she held in her hands. And just like the quilt she was fashioning, He'd woven a tapestry of joyful color in her own life.

An hour later, fatigue overtook her. Weary in body, but not in soul, Raelene drifted off to sleep with two thoughts on her mind. One came from the Bible: *"Christ is all, and in all."*

God was all she needed. As for the other, she couldn't wait to see Gustaf tomorrow to share her exciting news.

sixteen

The next morning, Gustaf was nowhere to be found. Raelene completed the morning farm duties, prepared a light meal to break the fast, and headed for her garden. Even the most mundane task seemed significant in light of her newfound joy. Yet she couldn't fully lose herself in tending to the plants and flowers. Her senses were on full alert for any sign of Gustaf's presence. She needed to confide in someone, and while her head told her it should be Cedric, her heart hoped for Gustaf.

Placing two fists at the small of her back to work out a few kinks, Raelene caught sight of a lone figure walking across the field from the Hanssen farm. A welcoming smile broke upon her lips. But the visitor didn't possess Gustaf's familiar swagger and was much too narrow in the shoulders. A fleeting twinge of disappointment turned to alarm as the person drew nearer.

Why was Fraya Hanssen coming to call this early in the morning? Raelene petitioned heaven, praying Gustaf's mother wasn't coming to bear bad news. *Wait*, she cautioned herself. She wouldn't give way to negative thoughts. How easily the natural instinct had returned. Besides, Fraya would be running if something were wrong.

Raelene washed her hands with the creek water in the bucket next to her and stood to greet her guest. Drying her hands on her apron, she paid close attention to Fraya's face. Although a smile was on her lips and in her eyes, concern creased her brow. This was more than a social call.

"Good morning, Miss Strattford. I come at good time, yes?"

Her accent was thicker than Gustaf's, and her clothing was

made with the same fine, even stitches as her son's, visible evidence of the loving care she gave to her family. Raelene folded the woman's hands in her own. "You have come at a most welcome time, Mrs. Hanssen. I am happy for the company."

Fraya tilted her head to the side and pursed her lips. "You have much weight on your mind. Something troubles you?"

Gustaf's mother was nothing if not direct. Now Raelene knew where Gustaf got that quality. Raelene thought about keeping her news a secret, but one look at the kindness and wisdom she saw in Fraya's eyes disarmed her. Perhaps another woman would better understand.

"No, nothing is wrong. In fact, quite the opposite. Come join me for tea, and I'll tell you all about it—if you have time," Raelene added.

"But of course, *min unge,*" the woman replied. "It is you I came to visit."

My little one. Raelene hadn't heard that endearment since Mama called her that as a little girl. It wasn't until she was seated at the table in her kitchen with a hot cup of tea in her hands that she realized how much she'd missed fellowship with another woman. As a new bride, Kaariana had been understandably occupied and absent from Raelene's farm, and with Mama gone, no one else was left.

Gustaf's mother settled on the bench opposite Raelene and rested her arms on the table. Her motherly demeanor touched Raelene's desperate longing. "Drink tea, and tell me your heart."

She was straight to the point, just like Mama. The accumulation of concerns that burdened Raelene's weary soul spilled like milk from an upended pail, thoughts flowing in every direction.

"I—I am not sure. I mean, I do not know," she babbled, trying to gather her thoughts into some semblance of coherency. "I hardly know where to begin."

"Maybe I help some?" the kindly woman asked. "My Gustaf tell me he see you at meeting last night. I think you have great anger and sorrow for long time. Now you have peace. I see its joy in your eyes."

Raelene could hardly believe it. All those emotions tumbling around inside of her, wanting release, and Fraya had summed it up in just a few words. Sometimes, a limited vocabulary proved beneficial. Meeting Fraya's gaze over the rim of her teacup, Raelene blinked back the tears that had gathered.

"I see everything the way Mama and Papa talked about, and the way Gustaf was trying to show me." She shook her head and wiped away the moisture from her cheek with the back of her hand. "And I do," she declared. "I *finally* have peace. And while I owe it all to the Lord, it was Gustaf who pointed me in the right direction. He would not give up. He would not let me wallow in my bitterness, even when I took it out on him."

Instead of acting surprised, Mrs. Hanssen nodded, beaming with motherly pride. "My Gustaf, he talks a lot about you."

No doubt to complain about how hard it was to work for someone like her or how stubborn she was. And he was so right.

"Yes, I can believe he does," Raelene ventured hesitantly.

"He sees your sadness but knew you do not want his help. And that hurts him." The regret in her tone turned to hope. "Maybe now things will change?"

Gustaf? Hurt by her actions and words? And she'd thought he was always angry with her. Although, as she thought back, there'd been a moment or two when she might have glimpsed hurt. He'd covered it so quickly with irritation that she hadn't been sure. Then he'd kept his distance as though to punish her.

"I'm so sorry, Mrs. Hansen. I truly would never intentionally hurt Gustaf."

"He care for you very much, you know."

That revelation shook her to the core. Care for her? After all she'd done to him? "You must be mistaken."

Fraya squared her shoulders. "I know my Gustaf."

Now she'd done it. Raelene should know better than to imply to a mother that she was wrong about one of her children. "Please forgive me, Mrs. Hanssen. I did not mean to imply that you do not, but Gustaf has not been very cordial to me lately. That is why I find the idea of him caring very difficult to believe."

Gustaf's mother placed a warm and comforting hand on Raelene's arm. "He try to hide it, but a mother know the heart of her son."

Raelene continued to ponder those words long after Fraya left. There had been times when Raelene thought Gustaf might have felt some of the same attraction that afflicted her, but he'd never made any move to confirm it. Besides, how could he possibly care about her if he was so eager to see her marry someone else? He'd all but shoved her at Cedric and given his blessing.

So what was she to think? She sighed. There was little left to do but wait on the Lord, as the Reverend Jonathan Edwards had said on Tuesday. Hopefully, *He* knew what was on Gustaf Hanssen's mind.

❧

Only two weeks remained until Raelene's eighteenth birthday, and she was about to despair of waiting. The corn and crops were harvested, and the amount of work around the farm had shifted to canning and preserving for the winter. Granted, they'd all been very busy. But no matter how hard she tried to strike up a conversation with Gustaf, he thwarted her every attempt.

"I have much work to do" or "You should speak with Mr. Milton" were his standard excuses.

Why was he being so difficult? If what his mother said was true, wouldn't he want to declare his feelings and save her from all this anguish? *Unless Fraya was wrong*, a contrary voice nagged her. Maybe he really wanted her to marry Cedric.

Whatever the man was thinking in that thick head of his, Gustaf's aloofness left a hole in her heart and life. It did help that Cedric was ready to fill it. He had become much more attentive in the past few days, and talk had turned increasingly to the future of her farm.

But he isn't Gustaf, she lamented, glancing to where Cedric stood by the bookshelf, tracing the outlines of the letters on the spines of the books. Awkward silence stretched between them, but Raelene had no heart for conversation.

"Miss Strattford, I. . ." Cedric cleared his throat and stepped around the table to stand before her. Stiff as a soldier at attention, he licked his lips several times, and his Adam's apple bobbed up and down with each swallow. Why was he so nervous?

"Mr. Milton," she interrupted, realizing that perhaps her extended silence was the cause, "before you say anything, I want to apologize for my behavior of late. I've been so distracted with the affairs of the farm that I have not been the most accommodating hostess. For that I am truly sorry."

Cedric clasped her hands in his. "My dear Miss Strattford, I find your company, even in silence, gracious and pleasurable at the very least. Indeed, I, too, have been distracted."

Curiosity at the sudden strength of his tone made Raelene meet his firm gaze. His thumbs lightly brushed the backs of her fingers, and the caress unsettled her.

"I know we have not known each other very long, but in the time we have spent together, I have found you to be a charming companion and someone for whom I hold deep respect."

"Yes, I feel the same way."

"And it could be even more," he ventured slowly.

Was he saying what she thought he was saying? She'd known this possibility existed, had thought about how she would respond when it happened; but now that the moment might be at hand, she was left with naught but a frozen wit and dry tongue.

"You will be eighteen next weekend, and I believe it is time that we make our relationship a more permanent one."

This was all Gustaf's fault. If only he'd let her know how he felt before now.

"We will make a great team, and this farm will thrive under our hard work. Miss Strattford, would you do me the honor of accepting my proposal of marriage?"

Or maybe he had.

Cedric's feelings toward her were clear. His proposal wasn't one buried beneath selfish ambition or personal gain like the others'. And while Cedric did seem to be preoccupied with the success of the farm, he readily offered to set aside his business affairs to see to her needs when the occasion had warranted it.

She should be happy. Excited, even. This was a moment she'd dreamed about all her life. But as she looked into Cedric's earnest gaze, the only face she saw was Gustaf's. Pulling her hands free, Raelene turned toward the fire. She finally had everything she needed to make her parents' dreams come true. And with the endless possibilities spread out before her, Gustaf prevented her from taking hold of them.

The heat from the fire warmed her face as the realization that it was Gustaf's hand next to hers as she took hold of those dreams. Despite her protests and attempts to keep her distance, one fact stood out with blinding clarity: She'd fallen in love with Gustaf Hanssen.

But he didn't want her.

Clawing past the dark despair cloaking that truth, she turned to face Cedric once again and conjured what she hoped was the right amount of exuberance for such an occasion.

"Yes, Mr. Milton, I accept your proposal of marriage."

Yet as she spoke, her heart felt as though it were folding, entombed within her chest.

❧

After the harvest was a popular time for weddings. Fresh fruits and vegetables were in abundance for the elaborate nuptial celebrations the colonists enjoyed. Raelene had always enjoyed the fall wedding season back home, and here was no different. Everyone in town would join together to turn the affairs into the social events of the year. Each one was planned to give the bride and groom, as well as their guests, a special memory to treasure long after the ceremony. . .even for a wedding that was nothing more than a business transaction.

Like hers.

At least on her part. While Cedric seemed to care for her, he couldn't conceal his preoccupation with the farm and the potential it offered. Conversations with him were always centered around the farm and how to increase production or profit. He hadn't made many attempts to get to know her or her interests, but he was always considerate of her wishes. Life could be worse.

More than ever, Raelene missed her midday conversations with Gustaf. The way he quietly lived his faith in every aspect of his life and his constant reminder that God hadn't abandoned her were the reasons she'd been receptive to Jonathan Edwards's sermon. And that had led to her turning back to God.

While Gustaf still saw to his duties, he no longer came to the cottage and avoided extended conversation.

Cedric's daily presence on the farm made the breech between Raelene and Gustaf feel as wide and cold as the

Christina River. Maybe it was just as well. She was getting married. Her heart and mind should be focused on her future, not dwelling on what would never be.

Raelene knew of three other weddings taking place, thanks to the banns posted at the town hall. Susanna, Doc's wife, had posted Raelene's for her parents in honor of their contributions to the growing settlement when they were alive. Thanks to Susanna's influence, every colonist within traveling distance of New Castle would most likely attend the wedding.

Moisture gathered in Raelene's eyes. If only she could feel a portion of the excitement reflected on the faces of everyone who gathered to help with preparations.

"Raelene, you are sad?" Kaariana's voice broke into Raelene's contemplation.

"I am worried we won't complete everything in time. Planning for the harvest and a wedding? My senses must be addled!"

Her best friend giggled, but concern quickly replaced the mirth. "But you are happy, yes?"

Happy? At knowing she wouldn't lose her farm, yes. But at knowing that in just a few days, she would marry Cedric? "Yes, I am," she said, as though to convince herself. "I merely have a lot on my mind. Forgive me for spoiling what should be a time of celebration."

Kaariana narrowed her eyes. Apparently satisfied, she returned to her work on the doilies that would grace the tables at the banquet after the wedding.

You will grow to love Cedric, Raelene told herself. His devotion to her and commitment to God would be enough. It had to be. Gustaf's avoidance of her made it clear she had no other option.

❧

Gustaf stood by as Cedric directed several men gathering

beans and corn. Mounds of cornstalks passed by in wagons as their neighbors worked together to divide the crops. It should be *him* giving the instructions and supervising the distribution of goods from their harvest. It should be *his* wedding the ladies were planning inside the cottage or during their afternoons in the orchard.

"Go to her," his mother had encouraged after her visit with Raelene almost two weeks ago. "Tell her you care."

As Gustaf recalled, that was the day after the meeting in town to hear Jonathan Edwards preach. The look of awe on Raelene's face was burned into his memory. And the pure joy in her eyes when their gazes had collided from across the room had filled his heart to overflowing. He'd been so close to going to her when he'd seen her glancing around. But she was on Cedric's arm. There was no room for him.

Cedric was everything Gustaf wasn't. Cedric was polished and well educated. Not only was he well versed in tending the land, but he was a man of means, genteel, like Raelene. His stories of London enthralled her.

Gustaf could never do that. All he could offer was love and a life of hard work. So he ignored both his mother's pleas to speak to Raelene and Raelene's attempts to speak to him.

These past few weeks working side by side with her had been nearly unbearable. Avoiding their midday conversations had left a hollow ache in his chest, and yielding the reins of the farm to her future husband had nearly choked the life from him.

Gustaf was glad that she'd finally come to grips with her anger at God and the pain of losing her parents, but that only made him love her more.

He stepped inside the barn before anyone noticed the searing glaze in his eyes. Yes, God help him, he loved her. There was no denying it. But she was tied to her land as Gustaf was tied to his promise.

As soon as she was wed, he'd head west, although the prospect of seeking his own land failed to excite him as it once did. Not without Raelene at his side.

"God help me," Gustaf mouthed as his heart twisted into a knot of anguish. *Help me to be happy for Raelene. Help me sacrifice my love for her happiness. Let the life she always wanted with an English gentleman be my last gift to her.*

seventeen

Raelene stood in front of the beveled glass mirror at the back of the church. The dark circles underneath her eyes gave evidence of her sleepless night. Indiscernible chatter and laughter floated on the breeze through the open door that faced the town green where final preparations for her wedding were taking place. Friends and neighbors and townsfolk bustled to and fro, there to celebrate what they assumed was a joyous occasion.

And it should be. It should be the happiest day of her life. She was eighteen, and she was getting married. Her groom waited anxiously to exchange vows with her. Afterward, they'd spend a full month at his home in the country before beginning their life together on her farm. But her heart would not go with them. It wasn't free to be given to Cedric. It belonged to a man who didn't want her.

Raelene smoothed her hands across the delicate pale blue brocade fabric of Mama's best gown. Originally a gown Mama had worn at court in England, it had a square neckline blended into a long train that hung from her shoulders. The lines of the bodice dipped to just below her waist, where it opened to reveal her cotton petticoats and panniers. She could've worn Mama's satin, but Raelene already felt overdressed in this country setting.

A tear escaped from one eye and traveled a slow path down her cheek as she examined the coiffure of blond curls Karianna had swept up with combs, leaving a lone curl to drape over her shoulder. "Oh, Mama. I wish you were still here. If you and Papa hadn't left me, everything would be different."

"I will never leave thee, nor forsake thee."

Raelene closed her eyes and shut out the distraction of the world around her. "Yes, God, I know," she whispered. "Your hand is in everything that is happening today. For that I am thankful."

How could it be that her soul was full when her heart was breaking?

"It is time, Raelene."

Raelene turned at the sound of Doc Schuylar's voice in the doorway. He was resplendent in his finest waistcoat and breeches, the buckles on his shoes polished to a shine and a new cocked hat adorning his head. Doc looked every bit the gentleman Papa would be if he were here to give her away. But that honor would go to next-best person, and Papa would have wanted it this way.

Mustering her courage, Raelene met Doc at the door and placed her trembling hand on his as he escorted her toward the town green. Those gathered blurred into a sea of unrecognizable faces. Briefly, she glimpsed Mr. Harvey from the town hall. But for the assembly's stipulation that she marry by today, she surely would not have accepted Cedric's proposal. The path she walked felt like it was bringing her one step closer to the executioner's block. And Cedric, dear Cedric, held the ax. As good as he was, perhaps she could grow to love him. After all, she hadn't loved Gustaf in the beginning.

Soft, haunting strains of a flute floated on the air as Doc led her down the aisle and placed her hand on Cedric's waiting arm. Her husband-to-be had selected a frock that would make the most fashionable men of London jealous. Yes, he cut a fine figure, and some women might consider him handsome. Yet somewhere along the way, Raelene had grown partial to wide shoulders clad in homespun and bronzed, sinewy arms bared to the elements.

When she turned to face her soon-to-be husband, she caught a glimpse of Gustaf. Leaning against a tree off to the side, his face partially concealed in the shadows, his focus was trained on her. All the determination in the world couldn't break the invisible bond that held their gazes captive. Even as she stood with the man she was about to marry, her heart bridged the distance to connect with that of another man. Heat warmed her cheeks in shame.

God, I'm trying to do the right thing, but I can't do it alone. Where are You? Maybe this was God's will. Maybe Gustaf wasn't the man she was supposed to marry. But God's will or nay, she couldn't dictate to her heart whom to love.

"If anyone here can show just cause as to why these two should not be joined in holy matrimony, let him make his proclamation known now or hitherto forever hold his peace."

The pastor's words doused Raelene's scrambled thoughts as effectively as water on a fire. She focused once more on the man standing opposite her and waited for what seemed an eternity for the ceremony to continue. Braving a glance at Cedric, she was surprised to see sadness in his eyes. Her heart hitched. Was he having second thoughts, as well? He closed his eyes, seemingly gathering strength or patience—she couldn't tell which—and cleared his throat.

"I'm—" He broke off.

What was he doing?

"I'm afraid that I must speak out against this sacrament."

The groom's protest sent waves of murmurs and whispers of shock among those in attendance. Raelene's lips parted in surprise. Tenderly holding her gloved hands in his, Cedric continued, his words only for her.

"My dear Miss Strattford, I cannot allow these proceedings to continue. It would be an injustice to the holiness of marriage and a travesty to force you to endure such a circumstance when your heart clearly belongs to someone else."

He knew? "But, Mr. Milton, I—"

Cedric released one of her hands and placed his fingers over her lips. "Do not attempt to dissuade me, my dear. I have been at the farm these past few weeks and have observed your attentions. They lie distinctly in your overseer's favor. While I regard you in high esteem, it is not my desire to force you into a life of unhappiness." Cedric shifted his gaze to the side briefly, implying that he knew of Gustaf's whereabouts. "I do not know why this gentleman has not made his feelings for you known," he said, returning his eyes to Raelene's, "but I must release you from your promise to me." He winced, as if it pained him to give her this freedom. "You are no longer bound by your word to marry me."

Raelene wavered between the elation of her freedom and dismay at the suffering that Cedric tried to hide behind a benevolent smile. She knew what he was feeling. He was a true gentleman. She didn't deserve him, but she did owe him her gratitude.

Pushing up on the balls of her feet, Raelene placed a chaste kiss on Cedric's cheek. When she pulled back, a look of surprise crossed his face.

"Thank you," she whispered. "You will make some lucky young woman very happy."

A wistful smile turned up the corners of Cedric's mouth. He gallantly bowed and stepped back. When he did, Raelene had a full view of Gustaf, standing as still and expressionless as a statue.

Heavenly Father, now what?

❧

Feet glued to the ground, Gustaf could hardly believe his ears. The *groom* objected to the marriage proceeding? Piece by piece, Gustaf's heart had started to break as the minutes passed and Raelene drew closer to pledging her life to another man. But now she stood facing him, no longer bound to Cedric Milton. As their gazes connected, neither one of them moved, but within his chest, Gustaf's heart pounded.

Doc's wife, Susanna, approached Raelene from behind and gave her a not-so-subtle nudge in his direction. Raelene jerked as though pulled from a daze. Ever so slowly, she moved in his direction. That freed his own legs from the mire of his shock. He walked toward her, meeting her halfway.

Standing in front of the woman he loved more than life itself, Gustaf couldn't talk. A mixture of apprehension, uncertainty, and a glimmer of hope crossed Raelene's face. She was no doubt waiting for him to make the first move, to set her doubts and fears aside. Gustaf looked over Raelene's shoulder at Cedric, who nodded encouragement. Gustaf knew this man was different from the others, as godly as he was noble.

"Do not just stand there gawking, man," Cedric said. "Say something to the lady."

Gustaf met Raelene's eyes once again. He wanted to speak, but how could he with a love-swollen heart in his throat?

"I love you." He mouthed the words stuck on his tongue, staring hopelessly at her brimming eyes.

Standing before him was everything his heart desired. He could have Raelene as his wife, work her farm, expand the cottage into a resplendent home fit for a queen, and raise a family to carry on his name. All he had to do was say what he felt.

He swallowed and tried to say the words again.

Nothing.

The ghost of a smile tugged at the corners of Raelene's mouth, giving Gustaf the strength and encouragement he needed. *Father in heaven, please let me get this right and not bumble through like an idiot.*

"Miss Strattford—"

"Mr. Hanssen—"

"I love you," they said together.

A becoming blush crept into Raelene's cheeks, and an overwhelming sense of relief released his heart from its constriction. How easy that had been. Why hadn't he done it sooner?

His ears rang with the cheers of celebration from their

friends and family gathered on the green. He'd almost forgotten about anyone else present, and she obviously had, too. Ever the demure lady, she fluttered her fan in front of her face, as though to hide her embarrassment.

With his large hand over hers, Gustaf stilled the rapid motion of her fan, staring over it and into her wide eyes.

"It appears as if we have a unique circumstance." The pastor spoke from what seemed like a world away. He cleared his throat. "Shall we amend the present festivities to be a celebration of your upcoming union, instead?"

Gustaf glanced at the pastor, then back at Raelene. "We have much to discuss, no?"

One lone tear slipped from Raelene's eye and began its descent on her cheek. Gustaf reached out and caught the tear, earning a warm smile from his beloved in return. She attempted to speak, but no words came forth. After several tries, she merely nodded.

The pastor clapped his hands together. "I see you are both in accord." He turned to address those gathered and raised his voice. "Let the merriment resume as we embrace the occasion of love discovered and anticipate the joyous union to come in a week's time."

He glanced across the crowd at Mr. Harvey, who gave an approving nod; the assembly would overlook the week's delay, and Raelene would keep her family's farm.

Although every part of him wanted to steal Raelene away and have her all to himself, Gustaf tucked her close to his side as they joined everyone in the celebration. Before they reached the tables, he leaned down and whispered in Raelene's ear. "Just seven days hence, we will be husband and wife. Never again shall we part."

Raelene nestled closer to his side, her silence saying so much more than words ever could.

epilogue

Raelene leaned back against Gustaf, his arms wrapped around her and their hands interlaced at her waist. The waning sun cast a warm glow over the gently sloping landscape of the farm, and stillness settled around them. As they stared out at the land that tomorrow would become theirs, a strong sense of peace washed over her.

"What thoughts dance in your head right now?" The vibrations of Gustaf's deep voice rumbled against her back.

"It is hard to believe that tomorrow is the day we wed. It feels like forever that we've waited for the day to arrive."

"Yes, but it is finally here. The days we have spent together talking about the future have been among the best I can remember. Everything we have done these past few months has brought us here."

His speech had improved remarkably. Raelene still had to catch herself each time she expected him to stumble over his words or use the stilted sounds that had endeared him to her. But being with her no longer made him uncomfortable.

"Den er fint så pass du del den hår time med jag."
It is good that you share this time with me.

As if in tune with her thoughts, he lapsed back into his native tongue. A thrill passed through her, and her mother's voice sounded in her head.

"Jag vill älska du för alltid."
Forever will I love you.

"Ja, and the same for me also." Gustaf leaned down and placed a soft kiss on her cheek. "A promise for tomorrow and for what is to come."

With the last rays of sunlight falling below the horizon,

Raelene watched Gustaf disappear over the hill toward his farm. Tomorrow they would pledge their hearts and their lives before friends and family. The path they had each traveled alone would be complete. From now on, they would walk the road together, side by side, as God intended. With her thoughts on that, Raelene wondered if she'd ever get to sleep.

>

As he had one week ago, Doc Schuyler extended his arm. Raelene placed her hand atop his. What a difference a week made. Where there had been hesitation, eagerness now hastened her steps. Gustaf had watched last week, knowing she wasn't happy. Now everything was different. Before he knew it, she stood facing him, the love in her eyes taking away his breath. How would he ever get through this?

God, please give me strength.

He reached for her hand and clasped it in his. Swallowing several times, he managed to find some semblance of his voice.

"Miss Strattford, I am not good with words. You know this. But I want to do this right." Gustaf removed his hat from his head, placing it over his heart. The action served to strengthen his resolve. Raising his voice for all to hear, he continued. "Our road has been long. We have had many bumps. But I want to make it smooth again and be by your side when the road is rough. We walk together. My love will carry you when you grow weary, and I will take care of you. This I promise."

Joy shone bright through a shimmer of tears in Raelene's eyes. She squeezed his hand. "Mr. Hanssen," she began in a whisper, then gained volume. "Despite my every foolish attempt to avoid it, my love for you crept in and filled my heart to a more bountiful abundance than I have ever known. It was your example, sir, that helped me lay aside my hurt and pain and take hold of the peace that our heavenly Father offers. Even when I was at my worst, your quiet faith spoke to me. It is the desire of my heart to share that faith. . .to walk with you through every storm and build a life together that honors God and our love. This I promise."

Gustaf replaced his hat and reached out toward Raelene's smooth brow, running his fingers across it and caressing her cheek. She leaned into his palm and closed her eyes.

"Let us continue." The pastor's voice interrupted their private moment. A giggle escaped from behind Raelene's lace-gloved hand. With an equally nervous chuckle, Gustaf nodded his consent in concert with hers.

"Very well, then." The man of God looked directly at Gustaf. "If you would loosen Miss Strattford's hair, we will proceed."

As was custom, Gustaf pulled Raelene's combs free. Her curls tumbled down her back, their ends brushing against her waist. With gentleness, he unraveled the braided portions and ran his fingers through her soft tresses, spreading the shroud of golden sunshine across her shoulders. All the while, Raelene held his gaze with her own, her eyes darkening with her love for him.

"Now for the ring," the pastor prompted, once they had exchanged their formal vows.

Gustaf stilled. He had no ring. He had forgotten to ask—

"Right here," Fraya Hanssen spoke up. His mother removed the ring from her right hand—his grandmother's ring—and handed it to him. "*Mormor* would be proud," she told him.

With a grateful smile, Gustaf took the ring. "Even if I was not so prepared, the Lord was, no?" he whispered softly as he slid the engraved gold band onto Raelene's left ring finger.

"And now"—the pastor cleared his throat and raised his voice so everyone gathered could hear—"by the authority granted to me by the New Castle Assembly, and inasmuch as Gustaf Hanssen and Raelene Krystina Strattford have pledged their troth to each other, I pronounce that they be man and wife together. Those whom God hath joined together, let no man put asunder. Amen."

The gathering heartily echoed his "amen," signaling their enthusiastic support.

After they recited the Lord's Prayer together, the reverend concluded the ceremony by saying, "And now, good Gustaf, you may kiss thy wife."

Wife. Gustaf cupped Raelene's face in his hands. He didn't think it was possible, but the joy of this moment made her even more beautiful. Slowly, he lowered his lips to hers. Her eyes fluttered closed. The softness of her mouth melted against his, as though their lips were meant for this. He shifted his arms to her back, pulling her closer, wishing this moment could last forever. Time seemed to stand still before he pulled away to observe the charming blush and recently kissed lips of his new bride.

Another round of cheers erupted. In a crush, the colonists circled in to offer their congratulations. Amidst the chaos, Gustaf and Raelene greeted everyone in turn before making their way toward the bounty of food set out for the celebration.

While everyone vied for a seat at the long rows of tables, Gustaf spirited his bride behind a copse of trees.

After another gentle kiss, he pulled Raelene close and tucked her head against his chest. "You make my heart happy," he murmured against her hair.

"As you do mine," she echoed. Pulling only far enough away to look into his face, she continued. "We have our love, our land, and God by our side. Every promise we have made has been fulfilled, and the promises made today will hold firm throughout eternity."

She was right, Gustaf realized. God had used the promises that brought them together against their will to bind them together forever. For as long as he lived, Gustaf would give thanks to God for letting a lady and a farmer find happiness, just like He promised.

A Letter To Our Readers

Dear Reader:

In order that we might better contribute to your reading enjoyment, we would appreciate your taking a few minutes to respond to the following questions. We welcome your comments and read each form and letter we receive. When completed, please return to the following:

Fiction Editor
Heartsong Presents
PO Box 719
Uhrichsville, Ohio 44683

1. Did you enjoy reading *Promises, Promises* by Amber Miller?
   ❏ Very much! I would like to see more books by this author!
   ❏ Moderately. I would have enjoyed it more if

   _____

   _____

   _____

2. Are you a member of **Heartsong Presents**?   ❏ Yes   ❏ No
   If no, where did you purchase this book? _____

   _____

3. How would you rate, on a scale from 1 (poor) to 5 (superior), the cover design? _____

4. On a scale from 1 (poor) to 10 (superior), please rate the following elements.

   ____ Heroine   ____ Plot
   ____ Hero   ____ Inspirational theme
   ____ Setting   ____ Secondary characters

5. These characters were special because? _____

_____

_____

6. How has this book inspired your life? _____

_____

_____

7. What settings would you like to see covered in future
   Heartsong Presents books? _____

_____

_____

8. What are some inspirational themes you would like to see
   treated in future books? _____

_____

_____

9. Would you be interested in reading other **Heartsong
   Presents** titles? ❑ Yes ❑ No

10. Please check your age range:
    ❑ Under 18   ❑ 18-24
    ❑ 25-34   ❑ 35-45
    ❑ 46-55   ❑ Over 55

Name _____

Occupation _____

Address _____

City, State, Zip_____

Hearts❤ng

Any 12
Heartsong
Presents titles
for only
$27.00*

HISTORICAL ROMANCE IS CHEAPER BY THE DOZEN!

Buy any assortment of twelve *Heartsong Presents* titles and save 25% off of the already discounted price of $2.97 each!

*plus $3.00 shipping and handling per order and sales tax where applicable. If outside the U.S. please call 740-922-7280 for shipping charges.

HEARTSONG PRESENTS TITLES AVAILABLE NOW:

(If ordering from this page, please remember to include it with the order form.)

Presents

Great Inspirational Romance at a Great Price!

Heartsong Presents books are inspirational romances in
contemporary and historical settings, designed to give you an
enjoyable, spirit-lifting reading experience. You can choose
wonderfully written titles from some of today's best authors like
Wanda E. Brunstetter, Mary Connealy, Susan Page Davis,
Cathy Marie Hake, Joyce Livingston, and many others.

When ordering quantities less than twelve, above titles are $2.97 each.
Not all titles may be available at time of order.

SEND TO: **Heartsong Presents Reader's Service**
          P.O. Box 721, Uhrichsville, Ohio 44683

Please send me the items checked above. I am enclosing $ _____
(please add $3.00 to cover postage per order. OH add 7% tax. NJ
add 6%). Send check or money order, no cash or C.O.D.s, please.

To place a credit card order, call 1-740-922-7280.

NAME _____

ADDRESS _____

CITY/STATE _____ ZIP _____

HEARTSONG
PRESENTS

If you love Christian romance...

$10.99

You'll love Heartsong Presents' inspiring and faith-filled romances by today's very best Christian authors. . .Wanda E. Brunstetter, Mary Connealy, Susan Page Davis, Cathy Marie Hake, and Joyce Livingston, to mention a few!

When you join Heartsong Presents, you'll enjoy four brand-new, mass market, 176-page books—two contemporary and two historical—that will build you up in your faith when you discover God's role in every relationship you read about!

Mass Market 176 Pages

Imagine. . .four new romances every four weeks—with men and women like you who long to meet the one God has chosen as the love of their lives...all for the low price of $10.99 postpaid.

To join, simply visit www.heartsong presents.com or complete the coupon below and mail it to the address provided.

✂- -

YES! Sign me up for Heart♥ng!